"Would you kis a hamburger?"

"I think my vegetarian taste buds could handle that," Willow answered.

Heath tilted her head back and kissed her. He deepened the kiss as her heart thundered in her chest.

"You don't know how long I've wanted to touch you," Heath said.

"Two days?"

"A lot longer than that. I was just a silly kid who didn't know how to approach the most fascinating girl I'd ever encountered."

Her lips twisted into a smile. "I'm sure your popular friends would've had a lot to say if you'd started dating the 'Tree Girl.'"

"Maybe. I wasn't as bold or independent as you. Following the clues to my mother's disappearance instead of doing my father's bidding is the closest I've come to rebelling against him."

"Is that what this is? Seducing me to get back at Daddy?"

"This is me seducing you—" he kissed her throat "—because I want you more than anything right now."

"Then be bold and independent and take me."

"Would you kiss me now, even though I just ate a hamburger?"

WHAT LIES BELOW

CAROL IMODO

WHAT LIES BELOW

CAROL ERICSON

Harlequin

INTRIGUE

Harlequin® INTRIGUE™

ISBN-13: 978-1-335-45693-9

What Lies Below

Harlequin Enterprises ULC
22 Adelaide St. West, 41st Floor
Toronto, Ontario M5H 4E3, Canada
www.Harlequin.com

Printed in Lithuania

MIX
Paper | Supporting responsible forestry
FSC® C021394

Carol Ericson is a bestselling, award-winning author of more than forty books. She has an eerie fascination for true-crime stories, a love of film noir and a weakness for reality TV, all of which fuel her imagination to create her own tales of murder, mayhem and mystery. To find out more about Carol and her current projects, please visit her website at carolericson.com, "where romance flirts with danger."

Books by Carol Ericson

Harlequin Intrigue

A Discovery Bay Novel

Misty Hollow Massacre
Point of Disappearance
Captured at the Cove
What Lies Below

The Lost Girls

Canyon Crime Scene
Lakeside Mystery
Dockside Danger
Malice at the Marina

A Kyra and Jake Investigation

The Setup
The Decoy
The Bait
The Trap

Visit the Author Profile page at Harlequin.com.

CAST OF CHARACTERS

Heath Bradford—A developer tasked with buying up property on Dead Falls Island for a casino project, Heath comes to the island with a different set of priorities, and meeting up with the "Tree Girl" only strengthens his resolve, even though his desire for the truth puts them both in danger.

Willow Sands—An ecobiologist, the "Tree Girl" loves the land she studies and protects, but an unlikely alliance with Heath Bradford puts them both on a path that could destroy them before it destroys the land they seek to preserve.

Toby Keel—Willow's neighbor winds up dead, and the police can't decide if his death is a homicide or an accident, but it does set off a chain of events that threaten Willow and her property.

Paul Sands—Willow's father left a complicated will that only serves to pit Willow against the man she's falling for.

Jessica Bradford—Heath's mother died under mysterious circumstances, and Heath's search for the truth leads him to a dark side of the island he loves.

Lee Scott—This member of the Samish Nation is its primary advocate for building a casino on the island, and he'll do whatever is necessary to achieve his goal.

Ellie and Garrett Keel—Toby's niece and nephew expected to inherit their uncle's property on his death and reap the rewards of its sale, but when a twist in the will disrupts their plans, they vow revenge.

Chapter One

Apollo sensed the intruder before she did. Willow Sands's dog cocked his ears forward. His nostrils twitched, and he let out a soft whine.

When a twig cracked, Willow sat forward in her camp chair and placed her hand on top of Apollo's broad head. "What is it, boy? Is that a coyote out there?"

Apollo's whine morphed into a growl in the back of his throat, and his fur stood on end. Coyotes didn't usually make Apollo nervous. Her Rottweiler might be old, but the coyotes in the area showed him respect, never encroaching on his territory.

Willow shoved her feet into her Birkenstocks and pushed up from her camp chair. Apollo's tail stirred up little eddies of dirt as he thumped it on the ground. "So, you're happy I'm investigating instead of you?"

Shuffling toward the tree line that ringed her property, Willow whistled through her teeth, the sound piercing the silent night. "Scram! And don't leave any rabbit carcasses around my cabin. Doesn't impress me."

Apollo had followed her lead and stood next to her, his body stiff, his fur tickling her leg.

She flicked his ear. "Don't go chasing after anything out there. I don't want to have to rescue you."

Typically, when Apollo sensed an animal in the woods, he'd bark to warn it off, as his hunting skills weren't what they used to be. When he sensed a human, he acted like this. On high alert but no barking, as if waiting for the person to make the first move.

Willow didn't like waiting for others to make the first move. She did better on offense than defense. Peering into the darkness, she shouted, "I don't want my dog chasing you, but I wouldn't mind some rabbit stew. Don't make me go for my rifle."

She was totally bluffing—not about the rifle; she had one and knew how to use it, but she'd never kill a rabbit or any other type of animal. Humans were the trespassers in the forest, not the rabbits or deer or coyotes or any of the other fauna that roamed the island.

Willow huffed out a breath after realizing she'd been holding it. Her release seemed to set the forest in motion, as a flock of birds winged it skyward and a chorus of crickets and frogs competed for dominance with their song. Beneath the cacophony, Willow detected branches rustling and some earthbound creature retreating along the carpet of dense, rotting organic material.

Apollo shook himself and circled back to his spot next to her chair. He collapsed, exhausted from doing his duty, his head shoved beneath the seat. If her dog no longer detected an interloper near their cabin in the woods, she could relax, too.

She scanned the forest one more time and then joined Apollo, plopping down in her chair. "We showed him, didn't we, boy?"

Apollo snorted, halfway to a snore, and Willow tried to roll the knots out of her shoulders.

When her heart stopped galloping, she wedged her feet against the rocks ringing her campfire and flipped open the notebook in her lap. She scribbled a few more notes in the margins of the table she'd worked on today while surveying the summer flora and fauna of Dead Falls Island, where she returned every June after her classes at the university ended. She'd grown up on the island in this very cabin, taking care of her father after her mom had left them.

She couldn't blame her mom for taking off. Mom had grown weary of Dad's drinking and mental instability—both of which worsened in the wake of Mom's departure. But Willow did blame her mother for leaving *her* behind.

Of course, Willow had always been closer to her father than her mother. If Mom had offered her a seat on the ferry that had carried her away from the island, Willow probably would've declined it anyway. Someone had to watch out for Dad.

That task had fallen to her until just after her eighteenth birthday, when she'd been debating whether or not she'd be able to attend the University of Washington, leaving Dad behind to fend for himself. Perhaps sensing her dilemma, Dad had made her decision easy by drinking himself to death that winter.

As she'd reached the legal age of adulthood, social services couldn't do anything about her decision to remain in this cabin to finish high school and then attend UW for what turned out to be a full ride.

Now she'd never give up this cabin, her land or the island—not to build something bigger and shinier and certainly not to those greedy developers who wanted to bring tourism to this side of the island, along with the Samish people's plans for a casino.

As she smacked her notebook shut, she startled Apollo, who jerked his head up. "Sorry to disturb your hundredth nap for the day."

When her dog lumbered to his feet and let out a loud bark, she realized she wasn't the one who'd awakened him. She dropped her notebook on her chair and jumped to her feet. Why had her cabin all of a sudden become the hot gathering place for all the critters in the forest?

Apollo put his nose to the ground, and she followed him to the tree line. He stopped, tilted his head back and barked again. This was more like his animal-alert stance.

"Keep barking, boy. If you get lucky, you won't have to give chase." As she scanned the tree line, a pair of gleaming orbs appeared among the bushes.

An animal edged into the clearing, and Apollo jumped into action, racing toward the creature. Willow tried to call him back, but when she saw Luna, Toby Keel's mutt, she stopped yelling at Apollo.

Willow crouched and whistled softly. "Come here, girl. Does Toby know you're out and about?"

The white dog of indeterminate lineage loped toward Willow. Luna's ears folded, and her tongue hung out of her mouth. She'd been a shy dog ever since Toby, Willow's nearest neighbor, rescued her from the bay. They both theorized that some holiday boaters must've tossed her overboard, so Toby made up for that abandonment by spoiling Luna every day. She rarely left his side.

Snapping her fingers, Willow said in a low voice, "C'mon, Luna. Did you get lost chasing something in the woods?"

As Luna made her way toward Willow, Apollo sniffed

the other dog. At least he'd stopped barking. Had Luna been skulking around the cabin before, too afraid to make herself known?

When Luna reached Willow, she nuzzled her outstretched hand and whimpered. Willow stroked her back. "What is it, girl?" Willow's hand skimmed across Luna's wet, sticky fur. She peered at her palm, stained with a dark substance. "What did you get into?" Hooking her fingers around Luna's collar, Willow pulled the dog toward the glowing light of the fire. She inspected the dog's fur and sucked in a breath. "Are you injured?"

Blood streaks marred Luna's fluffy coat. Willow ran her hands down Luna's legs, and she felt the pads of her front paws. Luna stood patiently while Willow used the flashlight from her phone to inspect the rest of her body. She couldn't find any injuries on the dog, but when Luna panted, the drool that hung from her jaws had a red tinge.

"Did you unleash on a rabbit?" Willow swallowed hard. Luna did not possess the hunting gene. She might give chase but wouldn't know what to do with a wild animal if she actually caught it. "Did you come across something dead in the woods?"

Not that Luna could answer her, but the better questions would be why had she left Toby's cabin and where was Toby? Willow wiped her hand on one of the rocks ringing her campfire, and then cupped that same hand around her mouth and shouted, "Toby? Toby, you out there? I have Luna."

Luna whined again as Apollo cocked his head, listening for an answer to Willow's call. No sound came from the forest, so Willow flipped over her phone and checked for a signal. Getting cell phone service on this side of the island was a dicey proposition, and Toby had his phone turned off most of the time, anyway.

Standing up, Willow held her phone in the air, but that last-ditch effort didn't fly out here. Wasn't that why she and Toby liked this location?

She shoved the phone in the back pocket of her jeans. "Looks like we're going to have to take a little evening stroll."

Willow headed into her cabin to grab a proper flashlight and yank a flannel shirt from a hook by the front door. She needed the long sleeves more as a buffer against the branches and spiky leaves in the forest than protection against the elements. June had ushered in a warm spell on the island, even at night. She tied the laces of her hiking boots and locked up.

Once outside, she flicked on the flashlight and stuffed her arms into the flannel, which she left unbuttoned over her T-shirt. She patted her thigh. "C'mon, guys. Let's take Luna home."

And find out why Toby hasn't come after his dog.

Toby Keel, a member of the Samish Indian Nation, had bought his property from her father for a song. Dad's family had been big landowners on Dead Falls Island. Slowly, the Sands family holdings had been parceled out and sold up. By the time her father inherited the family assets, the acreage on this side of the island comprised the last of the Sands land.

Paul Sands had no inclination to sell or develop his parcel of dirt. If Toby hadn't been Samish, her father never would've parted with the land. He always figured the Samish had more rights to the land than he did.

Shattered from his deployment during the Gulf War,

Willow's father wanted only to be left alone, and he'd found his perfect paradise at the edge of the forest on Dead Falls Island. He and Toby were two of a kind.

Willow's hiking boots crunched through the mulch on the forest floor as she trod the well-worn path between the two properties. Much like her father, Toby wanted to be left alone, so she obliged during the summer months when she took up residence at the cabin. But Toby's dog had arrived at her place smudged with blood. That necessitated an impromptu visit.

As they drew closer to the clearing for Toby's home, Luna picked up her pace and Apollo followed.

"Wait up, you two." In her haste to follow the dogs, Willow tripped over a rotting log, saving herself by wedging her hand against the nearest tree. The rough bark scraped her palm, and she rubbed the sting against the thigh of her jeans.

She slowed her pace as the dogs disappeared ahead of her. She didn't need a broken ankle out here. Aiming the flashlight at the ground, she picked her way over the tangled roots that marked the end of the path to Toby's cabin. He'd allowed the forest to encroach on his land even more than her father had, so the edge of Toby's cabin sat close to the tree line.

Willow's steps faltered as the dogs started barking furiously. Luna sent up a spine-tingling howl that hearkened back to her wolf ancestry, and Willow pressed a hand to her chest, where more than just physical exertion had her heart thumping against her rib cage. Something had clearly disturbed Luna, and Willow dragged her feet the final fifteen yards to Toby's clearing, dread pounding a beat against her eardrums.

When she parted the branches and peered at Toby's cabin, the flickering flames of his campfire cast a burnished glow on the dogs' fur as they circled the ground. She crept into the clearing. "Toby?"

Luna threw her head back and howled again. Willow felt like doing the same, but she proceeded to the other side of the fire where the dogs paced.

As she drew closer, Apollo turned and trotted toward her, allowing her to see Toby's body crumpled on the ground.

Gasping, she circled the fire and crouched beside him. She gripped his shoulder, shaking him. "Toby? Toby?"

Luna nudged Toby's head and came away with blood on her snout. That was when Willow noticed the cut on the side of Toby's head, and the sharp rock that lay inches from his scalp.

She pressed her fingers against his throat but couldn't feel a pulse. Had he tripped and fallen in a drunken stupor? Had a heart attack? A stroke?

As she fumbled for her phone, a low growl rumbled from Apollo's throat. Willow glanced up to see a dark figure coming from the other side of Toby's cabin, and she screamed loudly enough to rival Luna's howl.

Chapter Two

The woman's scream pierced his brain, and Heath Bradford tripped to a stop, his flashlight falling to the ground. The rolling light illuminated flashes of a woman on the ground, her mouth agape, and two big dogs circling her, barking and howling.

Heath dived for his flashlight and raised it, stalking toward the chaotic scene. He'd never hit a dog before, but he'd never encountered one attacking a human. He stomped his booted foot. "Get! Get out of here."

At the sound of his voice, the woman and the two dogs stopped their caterwauling and pinned him with three sets of eyes, two of those pairs gleaming in the dark. As the dogs no longer seemed to be menacing the woman, Heath lowered his flashlight and aimed it at the group.

That was when he noticed another figure sprawled on the ground behind the woman. He flicked the light over the prone form, and his pulse jumped. That had to be Toby Keel, and this did not look good. "What's going on? Does he need medical attention?"

The woman drew her knees up close to her body and wrapped one arm around her bent legs. "Who the hell are you, and what are you doing here?"

He hadn't expected that response, and his senses ramped up. Had he stumbled on a domestic? Had she just taken out Toby? He waved his free hand. "Hang on. Before we get to that, I think we should take care of Toby. Looks like he's out cold."

Her eyes narrowed as she jumped to her feet, one hand on the Rottweiler's head. "He's dead."

His hand tightening on the flashlight, Heath lunged forward. "Are you sure?"

Both dogs growled but stood their ground as he brushed past the woman and dropped to his knees beside Toby. He felt for a pulse, and then put his ear to the man's mouth, which was slightly ajar. His gaze flicked to the rock next to Toby's head and the blood soaking into the dirt.

"What happened to him?" Heath cranked his head around to take in the woman, standing stiffly behind him. Maybe he shouldn't turn his back on her.

"Good question." She folded her arms. "You tell me."

"Me?" He thumped his chest. "I just got here and found you and the dogs howling over a dead body. I'm completely in the dark."

"Same." She yanked on the Rottweiler's collar as the beast took a step toward Heath and the body. "His dog, Luna, came to my cabin about fifteen minutes ago with blood on her fur. Cell service being what it is out here, I decided to hike to Toby's to find out what was going on."

Understanding dawned on Heath, and he studied the woman standing before him, her spine erect, shoulders pulled back. Her dark hair swung from a high ponytail, random wisps framing the delicate features of her face. Shorter hair, riper body and attitude to spare, but he'd never mistake the Tree Girl for anyone else, even several years after he'd last seen her.

He wiped his hand across the chest of his flannel shirt and extended it to her. "You're Willow Sands, aren't you? Heath Bradford."

She went up on her toes like a startled doe prepared for flight. Then she tilted forward, thrusting her own hand toward his. "Right. I know you. Bradford and Sons Development."

If she spit the words at him, they couldn't have sounded more venomous coming from her lips. He expected that. When he took her hand in his, her slender fingers delivered a death grip. He *didn't* expect that.

When she released him, he flapped his hand. "Ouch. Quite a handshake you have there. Makes me think maybe you are strong enough to kill a man by smashing a rock against his head."

Her eyes widened, and she stepped back. "You think *I* had something to do with Toby's death? I told you. He was dead when I got here. Probably dead by the time Luna made it to my place."

He nodded. He didn't really think the Tree Girl was capable of murder. She probably avoided stepping on ants. "We need to get to someplace that has cell service and call the cops. Regardless of how Toby died, he is dead."

Stuffing her hands inside the arms of her shirt, Willow asked, "Do you really think someone bashed him on the head? I sort of figured he hit his head on that rock in a fall. Toby had heart issues…and drinking issues. I know that."

Heath lifted his shoulders. "Probably, but that's for

the cops to figure out. My vehicle is parked on the road behind Toby's cabin. You know better than I, but we should probably be able to get service from the road. I'll take you and the dogs."

"Luna's bloody, Apollo's dirty." Her lips twisted. "You sure you want them in your nice ride?"

"My truck is no stranger to filthy animals. My two Labs like frolicking in the river—mud and fur everywhere." He jerked his thumb over his shoulder. "I'm sure you know the way. Will Luna leave Toby's side?"

"She did before." Willow tugged her dog's collar and whistled. "C'mon, Luna. You can't help Toby now."

Luna snuffled around the body and planted herself next to Toby. Heath said, "I don't think she's leaving him this time."

"Doesn't look like it. I'll lead the way back to the road."

Willow stepped past him, and Apollo's tail thwacked Heath's leg as the dog curled his lip. Didn't seem Willow's dog liked him any more than Willow did.

Their two flashlights picked out the trail beneath their feet as they wended their way to the road that wound behind Toby's property. Heath clenched his teeth as he followed Willow. Just his luck that Toby would die right before their meeting. What were the odds of that happening? Heart issues. Who knew? Maybe the thought of discussing business with someone from Bradford and Son had stressed the guy out.

Heath crimped the edges of the note in his pocket. Or maybe it was that other business.

He glanced at Willow's swinging ponytail and huffed out a breath. Bradford and Son would have to shelve the notion of developing this side of Dead Falls Island. If his father thought Toby Keel would be a tough sell, wait until Heath told him about Willow Sands. Of course, that might depend on who just inherited Toby's property. They could still develop with one parcel, but definitely not without the two adjoining pieces of land.

As they emerged from the forest, Willow called back, "I see your truck. We can try our phones now."

Heath plucked his phone from the front pocket of his shirt and checked the bars on his display. "Not yet. Do you have the number for the Dead Falls Sheriff's Department, or should we call 911?"

"I've got their number." She stamped her boots on the asphalt and held up her phone. "And I've got service. I'll make the call."

While Willow called the DFSD, Heath scratched a spot behind Apollo's ear, trying to get on his good side. The dog looked too old to do much damage with an attack, but Heath had other reasons for currying favor with Apollo. If the beast liked him, maybe his owner would soften toward him. Maybe she wouldn't capitulate enough to sell her land to Bradford and Son, but she might agree to dinner.

A guy could hope.

She ended the call and spun around. "They're coming out. The sheriff himself is on the way. New guy, who's supposed to be proactive."

As she started to plunge back into the trees, Heath held up a hand. "Why don't we wait in my truck? We can lead the sheriff to Toby's body when he gets here. I've got some water, some wipes for your hands."

Willow turned her palms up and gaped at the blood streaks staining them. "I—I didn't realize…"

"I don't know if you've recovered from the shock of finding Toby and then seeing me materialize in the darkness. I know I scared you by showing up." He touched her arm. "Why don't you have a seat in my truck before the sheriff arrives?"

Her shoulders sagged, and she sniffled. "I can't believe he's dead. I mean, he was kind of cantankerous, not too friendly, but every summer I knew he was on the other side of the forest from me."

"Come on." Heath jingled his key ring. "We've both had a shock."

And a disappointment. He pivoted toward his truck parked up the road from the trailhead and heard her footsteps shuffling behind him. When he reached his vehicle, he put down the tailgate. "Will Apollo jump in?"

"It's too high, and he's too old."

He opened the passenger door, leaving it wide as he circled around to the driver's side. As Willow hopped into the seat, her dog collapsed on the ground beside the truck. Heath twisted around and reached into a cooler for two bottles of water. He handed both to Willow. "One for you and one for Apollo, if he'll drink from the bottle."

"Thanks." She took one. "He can drink from mine. Don't you want one?"

"I'm not thirsty. Looks like you two need it more than I do."

She grabbed the second bottle and pressed it against her cheek. "Everything happened so fast. I think Toby's death is hitting me now."

"Yeah, honestly, you seemed more concerned with my presence there than you did with Toby."

She whipped her head around. "I'd already checked

Toby. I knew he was dead. What I didn't know was what you were doing near his cabin while his body lay on the ground. You still haven't answered that question."

"Toby and I had a meeting scheduled for nine o'clock tonight."

Taking a gulp of water from the bottle, Willow raised her eyebrows. "Odd time to take a meeting."

"His choice." Heath spread his hands. "I offered him a lunchtime meeting, dinner, cocktails at the Harbor Restaurant and Bar. He chose his cabin at nine o'clock."

"And because Bradford and Sons wants his land, you jumped." She snorted. "He was just toying with you. Toby was never going to sell that piece of real estate."

"I proposed the meeting, and he agreed." Heath shrugged. "I guess I won't know if he was toying with me or not."

Toby had another reason for meeting with Heath, but Tree Girl didn't need to know about that.

With the bottle halfway to her mouth, she jerked her hand, and the liquid spilled down her front. "Now that he's dead, his heirs can do whatever they want with the property."

"Whoever they are." He pointed at Apollo. "I think he wants some water."

"Sorry, boy." She cracked open the other bottle and tipped it for him to drink. He took the bottle opening between his teeth and took probably one sip for every two that dripped from his jowls.

Patting Apollo's head, she said, "Am I next on your list? I know what Bradford and Sons wants."

"Son."

"What?"

"Son. It's actually Bradford and *Son,* singular." He raised his hand. "I'm it. One son."

She studied his face, as if trying to catch him in a lie. "That's right. You were a few years ahead of me in school—before you went to some posh boarding school—and I don't remember that you had any siblings. Only child…like me."

"I think for similar reasons." He clenched the steering wheel. He didn't know why, but he felt cut off from the world here in his truck with the Tree Girl, as if they were the only two in the forest.

She snorted. "Was your dad an unstable alcoholic, too?"

"My father…" He was saved from explaining anything about his father by the rotating red-and-blue lights that approached them from behind. "Sheriff's here. What's his name?"

"Sheriff Chandler." She stepped out of the truck, nudging Apollo with her foot. "Don't bite the sheriff."

Heath followed her and introduced himself to Sheriff Chandler after Willow greeted the man. A patrol car pulled behind the sheriff's SUV.

After a handshake, Chandler nodded. "Heath Bradford—I know the name. You're a client of Astrid Mitchell's, aren't you? Interested in the Misty Hollow property."

Heath gave the sheriff a tight smile as he felt Willow's stare burning a hole in his cheek. The island hadn't changed since the time he'd spent here—small-town gossip got around quickly. "That's right. Astrid showed me the property the other day, and it has a lot of potential."

"Potential for what?" Willow wedged a hand on her

hip. "You do know that's the site of a family massacre, don't you?"

"I've been informed." He pointed to the trailhead. "Toby's cabin is this way, Sheriff. We had a meeting scheduled for nine o'clock tonight. I arrived a little late and found Willow screaming and the dogs barking."

"I'll lead the way." Willow looked over her shoulder and said, "And I didn't start screaming until I saw you lurking behind his cabin."

Chandler asked, "Why'd you scream, Willow? Did Heath startle you, or did you suspect some foul play regarding Toby's death?"

"Foul play? I don't think so." She tossed her ponytail over her shoulder. "Toby does have a head injury, but he's lying beside a rock. Looks like he could've fallen and hit his head on it. He's had heart issues for the past few years, and a drinking problem for longer than that."

As Heath was bringing up the rear with the two patrol officers behind him, Chandler turned to look back at him. "Is that what you saw, too? Head injury, rock, blood?"

"Yeah, same. The only weird thing I noticed was his lack of footwear."

"He was barefoot?" Chandler tripped over a root and righted himself by grabbing a branch. "Did you notice that, Willow?"

"I did, but I didn't think it was unusual. It's the beginning of summer. It's not hot, but it's definitely not cold. Toby's accustomed to this weather. If he was barefoot in his cabin and then came outside to do something, he might not put shoes on. I've seen him walking around outside with no shoes before."

"Okay. We'll take a look. I called for an ambulance. Next of kin?"

Willow answered, "Toby was divorced a long time ago, no kids, but he does have a niece and nephew. They're probably his closest relatives. Toby is Samish, but the niece and nephew don't live here on the island. They left the rez after high school. His brother, their father, is dead, as far as I know."

"Okay. Maybe he has something in his cabin that will allow us to contact them, or we can get the info from his phone. Do you know the names of the niece and nephew?"

"Ellie and..." Willow snapped her fingers. "Can't remember the nephew's name."

"Garrett." Heath kicked a rock out of his way with the toe of his hiking boot. "Garrett Keel."

Chandler said, "Thanks. That's helpful."

Heath ignored the intense look from Willow's green eyes as she turned to stare at him over the sheriff's shoulder. If Sheriff Chandler didn't care how he knew that nugget of information, he didn't owe anything to Willow Sands.

Heath kept his eyes down and his mouth shut the last several yards of the trail. When they broke through to the clearing, Toby's dog, Luna, barked at them from her position next to Toby's body.

"Was the dog here before?" Chandler approached the mutt, his hand held out.

"I told the dispatcher that's how I found Toby," Willow said. "Luna came to my place. She followed me back, and Heath and I left her here. She wasn't budging."

"Do you think she'll come to you now?" Chandler

had reached Luna, and she sniffed his hand. "I'd like to have a look at the body, take some pictures."

"Luna." Willow made kissing sounds with her lips.

Heath swallowed. He'd follow that sound anywhere, and Luna agreed with him. The dog peeled herself away from her owner's body and trotted toward Willow.

She grabbed the dog's collar. "You stay with me, girl."

Chandler took charge of the scene, ordering Heath and Willow to stand back with the dogs and telling his deputies to enter Toby's cabin. "Make note of any disturbances in there and see if you can locate a cell phone. Doesn't seem to be one with the body."

Heath straddled a picnic table bench and slid his fingers beneath Luna's collar. "I'll hang on to her. You already have your hands full with Apollo."

Willow released Luna's collar as soon as her fingers met his and rubbed them on the thigh of her jeans as if he had cooties. "Are you really interested in buying the Misty Hollow property?"

"It's a prime piece of real estate. I'd tear down the house and outer buildings, just like anyone would, I assume."

"Prime piece of real estate for what purpose? I thought Bradford was done developing that side of the island and had set its sights on this side."

"Misty Hollow isn't part of our plan. I'd be buying it for personal reasons." When he came back to Dead Falls Island this time, he discovered he'd missed it. Now, after seeing Willow Sands again, he missed it even more.

He'd had a thing for Willow in high school, but she hadn't socialized with his group of friends. She hadn't socialized at all. She'd lived with her father and spent most of her time in the woods, collecting specimens, cataloging, photographing. The other kids shunned her for what they deemed her *weirdness*, but she'd always intrigued him.

Sheriff Chandler stood up and called out for his two deputies, still inside Toby's cabin. "Stop what you're doing and secure this area. I think we've got a murder scene here."

Chapter Three

A chill snaked up Willow's spine, and she jerked away from Heath, who was sitting way too close to her. "M-murder?"

"I have to call in some resources, and I need you two to leave the scene. Drop by the station tomorrow, so I or someone else can take your formal statements."

Heath pushed to his feet, his fingers still curled around Luna's collar. "What makes you think there was foul play, Sheriff?"

"Rather not discuss that right now. Can one of you take Toby's dog?"

Willow licked her dry lips. "I think she'll come home with me."

"Thanks." Chandler dismissed them, turning to his wide-eyed deputies and giving them instructions.

"I'll give you a ride back to your place." Heath leveled a finger at the trail where one of the deputies was heading with his phone.

Her mind still whirling from Sheriff Chandler's news, Willow rose unsteadily to her feet. "I can walk back through the woods to my cabin."

He raised his eyebrows, and one disappeared beneath a lock of dark hair that curled over his forehead. "Toby may have been murdered—probably moments before you discovered him. I don't think it's a great idea for you to be plunging into the forest in the dark with two spooked dogs as your only protection."

Willow's gaze traveled to the tree line on the other side of Toby's property that led to her cabin. The path she took couldn't even really be called a trail. She hated to admit it, but Heath had a point. Toby's killer could still be wandering around.

Was Heath anxious to get her away from the scene of the crime? Did he want to grill her about what she saw? Why had he been coming from behind Toby's cabin instead of the end of the trail?

She scooped in a deep breath. Heath Bradford might be a scummy, money-grubbing developer, but she had a hard time envisioning him as a killer—and it wasn't just because he was so damned attractive.

She'd witnessed Heath's sensitive side more than once when they were young and he still lived on the island. She'd even seen him off on his own crying once—although she'd never told anyone, especially not him. She'd thought his grief had to do with his mother disappearing, just like hers did. Maybe that was what he meant by their similarities.

Ever since that day, she'd watched him, taken notice. Not that the very handsome, very popular Heath Bradford would ever give the Tree Girl two minutes of his time back then.

"Well?" He tugged on Luna's collar. "You might also have a hard time getting Luna away from here."

"You're right. I'll take the ride, but only if you fess up and tell me how you knew the name of Toby's nephew." She waved her hand in the air. "We're leaving, Sheriff Chandler. I'll be in touch tomorrow."

Heath called to the sheriff, "Me, too."

Chandler gave them a thumbs-up and returned to examining the area around Toby's body. Willow gave a little shiver. "I can't believe Toby was murdered. It's not like he has anything worth stealing."

"Maybe Chandler's wrong. He's gotta err on the side of caution and secure the scene just in case." Heath hung back at the trailhead and pointed his flashlight at the ground. "Lead the way."

They said little on their way back to the road and Heath's truck. He had a struggle on his hands with Luna, leading her down the trail. She seemed reluctant to leave Toby, and Willow's heart hurt for the dog.

When they got to the truck, Heath lowered the tailgate and Luna jumped inside. "Will Apollo let me pick him up and will he stay in the truck bed once I get him there?"

"I'm sure he will, but he's a solid dog. Don't let his age fool you."

Heath crouched down and gathered Apollo around the middle. With the dog's legs dangling, Heath hoisted him into the truck bed. When both dogs were settled, he stroked them both, murmuring in a low voice, before closing the tailgate.

He opened the door for her and went around to the other side. Punching on the engine, he said, "Tell me where to go."

As her mouth quirked into a smile, he jerked his head toward her. "I saw that. I meant literally give me directions."

She slid a sideways glance at him. "You know, you're not going to be very popular here, trying to develop this side of the island."

"You'd be surprised. We have a lot of support. The Samish are looking to cash in with a casino on the island."

She pulled her mouth down in a sad face. "Nobody I know is in favor of that. Besides, the Samish Reservation is on the other side of the island."

"They hold a plot on this side, too. The properties could dovetail—casino on Samish land and hotels and restaurants on Bradford land." He shrugged. "That kind of development would benefit their casino."

"Oh, I get it now." She tapped the window with her fingernails. "Toby's property and mine sit between the Bradford holding and the Samish land. Am I right?"

"Yours, Toby's, a couple of others."

She squinted at him in the darkness of the cab. "Is that how you know Garrett Keel? Have you already spoken to him?"

"I haven't spoken to Garrett. I just know he's on the title of the property with his uncle. We make it our business to know who we have to deal with. With Toby the one living here, we figured it was best to talk to him first."

"Might as well start with the hardest nut to crack, right?"

Heath's teeth flashed white in the low light, and she poked him in the thigh. "What's so funny?"

"We never figured Toby would be the most stubborn." He flicked a finger at her. "That would be you."

She snorted. "I'll save you the trouble, Bradford and *Son*. I have no intention of selling my property to you or anyone else—especially not to someone ready to destroy the ecosystem of the forest and put up a bunch of horrid hotels and cheap restaurants."

"We've developed other areas with the environment in mind, actually enhancing the habitat for the plants and animals and protecting them from wildfires and other natural disasters. Some of our resort areas have actually seen an increase in the population of some species." He stopped to take a breath and glanced at her face. "Not buying it, huh?"

"Is that the pitch you were planning for me?" Tilting her head, she wrapped her ponytail around her hand. "What pitch did you have in store for Toby? Were you going to tell him all his Samish brethren were on board for the casino? That he'd be impeding progress for the Samish Nation?"

"Close." He adjusted his mirror to check on the dogs when she told him to take the next turn. "You don't even live here, right? Aren't you a professor at the University of Washington?"

Her heart did a little skip that he'd kept tabs on her, but the euphoria fell flat when she reminded herself that he would know all about her just like he knew all about Toby Keel. "I am, but I'm writing my second book on this area and return often for research. I've been coming back to Dead Falls Island every summer since my dad passed away."

"I was sorry to hear about your father."

His softened tone made her nose tingle, and she drew the back of her hand across the tip. "Ah, you mean you weren't one of the ones to nod sagely and opine that Paul Sands, the resident eccentric of Dead Falls Island, had cirrhosis of the liver coming to him."

"Not at all." The truck bounced as Heath took it down the final unpaved stretch to her cabin. "And your dad wasn't eccentric. He was a fascinating man with a vast scope of knowledge behind an eccentric manner."

He threw the truck into Park, and Willow sat still in the idling vehicle, staring at Heath's chiseled profile. "You knew my father?"

"I wouldn't say I knew him. I'm not sure anyone really knew your father, but I talked to him many times while I lived on the island. He was generous with his time." He cut the engine. "I'll help you with the dogs."

Willow opened and closed her mouth. She wanted to ask Heath under what circumstances he had talked to her father, but he didn't seem inclined to share. Her father certainly never told her he'd had conversations with her secret high school crush.

When Heath cranked open his door, the noise startled her into action, and she grabbed the handle of the passenger door and shoved it open. By the time she circled to the back of the truck, Heath already had the tailgate down and Luna had jumped out of the truck and was sniffing the ground.

Leaning into the truck bed, Heath coaxed Apollo, "C'mon, old boy. You don't have to jump."

Willow blurted out, "Where are your dogs now? Home with the wife and kids?"

Heath clicked his tongue softly, luring Apollo to the edge of the truck bed and then scooping him up and lowering him to the ground. "They're at my house in Seattle with my buddy's college-age daughter, who's dog- and house-sitting for me. I'm sure she's spoiling them."

No wife and kids. She closed her eyes and eked out a small breath. That wasn't too obvious at all. "Thanks for the ride and the help with Apollo. I'll be going to the station tomorrow to give my statement."

"Whoa. Wait a minute." Heath stood in front of her cabin, turning in a circle, his arms outstretched. "You're out here on your own?"

"I have Apollo." She rubbed her knuckles on the top of her dog's head. "And now Luna."

"Luna couldn't help Toby, and no offense to Apollo, but it looks like his personal protection days might be behind him." To lessen the blow, Heath cuffed Apollo's ears, his fingers running over Willow's.

She snatched her hand away from Apollo's head and Heath's electric touch. Must be all those unresolved adolescent issues. She cleared her throat. "I also have a few weapons, and they're loaded and ready to go."

"The Tree Girl is locked and loaded?" Heath widened his eyes in mock surprise.

"Tree Girl? Wow. I haven't heard *that* name in quite a while."

Heath covered his mouth with one hand. "Sorry. I didn't mean that as an insult. I've always thought of you that way."

Always? He always thought of her?

She waved a hand in the air. "I don't care. Didn't care back then, either."

Heath ran a hand through his hair. "I—I'm sorry. I mean it as a compliment, not an insult."

Laughing, she said, "Forget it. Just haven't heard anyone call me that in years."

"Understandable. Just know I didn't use it to insult you, and I'm relieved that you have firearms. Keep them handy tonight. It'll make me feel better about leaving you out here on your own."

"I'll be fine. Apollo may not look like much these days, but he's still a good watchdog." She nodded toward her dog, now collapsed at Heath's feet, his head resting on his hiking boot.

"So, he'll at least alert you if someone's in your area." Heath wiggled his foot. "When he wakes up."

"Yeah…" She stopped and caught her lower lip between her teeth. Had there been someone near her cabin earlier, before Luna showed up? About the time Toby died?

Cocking his head, Heath said, "What's wrong? Can we count on Apollo to keep watch?"

"Yeah." She shook her head. "Yeah, he can handle it. You'd better head back to your hotel and let the rest of the suits at Bradford and Son know that your meeting with Toby didn't work out the way you wanted it to… or maybe it did."

"Hey, that's a low blow. We wanted the guy's property for a fair price, not his death."

"But his death makes it more likely you'll get that property."

"Not necessarily. I don't know a thing about Ellie or Garrett Keel."

"Except their names."

"Yeah, well, names alone don't tell if they're going to be any more willing to sell the property than their uncle." Heath brushed his hands together. "You know what? I gotta go. You be careful out here."

He turned on his heel before she had a chance to respond. She guessed she deserved that. She'd practically just accused him of murdering Toby to get his land.

When Heath cranked on his engine, she shaded her eyes against the headlights flooding her yard and waved. She couldn't see if he responded or even saw her.

She sighed and scratched Luna behind the ear. "C'mon, you two. It's probably better to have an adversarial relationship with Heath Bradford if he's trying to develop this side of the island. No fraternizing with the enemy."

Apollo whined as he sat at her feet while she unlocked the door to her cabin. "And that means you, Apollo. I saw how you were looking at him."

After she settled Apollo and Luna in side-by-side beds in the living room, she yanked open the door to the closet by the front door and grabbed her father's pump-action Remington. He'd taught her how to use it, and she cleaned and loaded it at the beginning of each summer visit.

She'd never slept with it beside her bed—until now. Placing the rifle on the floor next to her, she slid between the sheets. If Toby was murdered and his killer got any bright ideas about her, she'd be ready for him. She *wasn't* ready for Heath Bradford.

THE FOLLOWING MORNING, not one dog but two woke her up. Willow scrambled out of bed and opened the front door for them. She didn't know Luna's routine, and until she had time to learn it, Toby's dog would have to follow Apollo's schedule.

As the dogs sniffed around outside, Willow put away the shotgun. It had made her feel safer after last night's events. When she went to the DFSD today, she'd nose around a little to find out if Sheriff Chandler had decided Toby's death was a homicide.

Hard to believe anyone would want to kill Toby, but then, she didn't know much about the man's past before he bought that property from her father and took up residence there. The guy preferred to be alone, so something or someone must've driven him to that solitude.

She shook out enough dog food to fill two bowls and set them outside on the porch. As she gazed out at the tree line ringing her house, an eerie feeling settled on her skin. Who or what had been out there last night before Luna showed up? Could it have been Luna sniffing around before she made her presence known?

Willow dipped back into the house to grab her long-sleeved flannel from last night and stuff her feet into her hiking boots. The dogs didn't even look up from their breakfast as she ducked through the opening that led to the path to Toby's cabin.

The tree canopy shadowed the ground, but enough light seeped between the branches that she didn't need a flashlight to see. She took the same path she'd hiked last night after Luna showed up, taking her time and looking for snapped twigs and trampled undergrowth. She discovered a little of both.

Had something or someone come this way last night, or were these the signs of her own trek through the forest? She glanced up after stepping over a complex root system blocking her path, and something red flapping from a tree branch caught her attention.

She made a beeline for the Pacific madrone and reached out for the piece of cloth hooked on a small branch jutting from the reddish trunk. She rubbed the flannel material between her fingers. It had come from a shirt, most likely.

She held the bit of cloth to her nose and sniffed, and

then smoothed it against her palm. This clean, fresh-smelling piece of fabric hadn't been out here long.

The hair on the back of her neck quivered. The material had probably been here since last night—when someone had been watching her cabin.

Chapter Four

Heath grabbed his red flannel shirt from the hanger in the closet and tossed it over the back of a chair. The meteorologists on TV had been predicting a warm start of the summer months on Dead Falls Island, but when it came to the islands of Discovery Bay, warm was relative.

His father, vacationing with his new wife, hadn't been happy when Heath told him about the complications with Toby. His old man would be even less happy to discover Heath's other business with Toby.

Even though Dad had also ordered him to track down the niece and nephew and start working on them, Heath decided he'd wait a few days before approaching the relatives. If Sheriff Chandler did rule Toby's death a homicide, Toby's family would be in shock and grieving. Not the best time to bring up a land deal. But minutiae like murder never stopped his father.

He checked his phone for messages, thought about texting Willow to find out if she'd made it through the night okay and then just as quickly discarded that idea. Not only did his company and business disgust her, she also had him pegged as a killer.

Had he really called her Tree Girl to her face? He

didn't need to give her more reasons to dislike him, but he was batting a thousand.

His stomach grumbled when he left his hotel room, but he wanted to get to the sheriff's station to give his statement before he did anything else. He didn't exactly have an alibi for the time of Toby's…death, but the GPS on his truck should show the time he arrived at Toby's place. He wanted to get in the clear with Chandler in case the sheriff had the same line of thought as Willow.

He tucked the phone into his pocket and grabbed the flannel on his way out of the hotel room. He drove through the town of Dead Falls and along the winding coastal road to the sheriff's station.

When he got out of his truck, he gazed at the harbor and bay below the cliff. The station had one of the best views in town. The land would be worth a lot of money today—almost as much as Toby's.

As he pushed through the door of the station, he almost ran straight into Willow, dressed in jeans and boots again—not that the casual look didn't suit her. He had a hard time dragging his gaze from her fit body to meet her eyes.

"Sorry." He held out a hand as if to steady her, but the cold look in her green eyes ended that courtesy. "Everything okay last night? Luna good?"

She tugged on the flannel he grasped in one hand. "I don't think you'll need this today."

He flattened the crumpled shirt against his chest with his arm. "I remember island weather as unpredictable. Are you all right?"

"I'm good, yeah." She rubbed her palms on the thighs of her jeans. "Luna seems to want to go back to the scene of the…Toby's death, but I've been distracting her. You here for your statement?"

"I am. Happy to hear Luna's doing okay. Let me know if you need any help with her." He took a step away from her and the weird vibe emanating from her stiff frame.

Reaching out, she grabbed his sleeve. "Do you mind if I wait for you while you give your statement? Th-there's something I want to ask you. It shouldn't take you too long. I'll buy you breakfast or a coffee when you're done."

He schooled the surprise out of his face. She wanted to buy him a meal? She looked like she wanted to stab him with a small, sharp object. "Sure, you can wait. I could use something to eat. How long were you in there?"

"About fifteen minutes."

"Did the sheriff give away anything about Toby's death?"

"Nope." She tilted her head and a cascade of auburn-tinted brown hair fell over her shoulder. "He's going to check out your alibi."

"He probably will. He can look at the GPS on my truck, so he can try to pin down the time of death or at least some kind of timeline." He leveled a finger at her. "Did he check yours, too?"

"Moi?" She slapped a hand against her chest. "I didn't have any reason to kill Toby."

"Yeah, well, neither did I." He cocked his head toward the front counter. "I think they're ready for me."

"See you when you get out."

As Heath walked through the swinging doors to the offices in the back, he glanced over his shoulder. Willow sank onto a chair in the lobby, the calculating look still playing across her face. He didn't know why he should have breakfast with a woman who suspected him of murder. Maybe he just wanted to prove her wrong. Maybe he just wanted to prove something to Willow so she'd stop eyeing him like a bug. Wait, no. She liked bugs a helluva lot more than she liked him.

His conversation with Chandler didn't last even fifteen minutes. He repeated what he'd told the sheriff last night and offered to share his GPS data with him. Chandler didn't give any hint which direction the investigation was headed and was impervious to Heath's hints.

As Heath stood to leave, the note from Toby burned a hole in his pocket. Should he share it with Chandler?

The sheriff asked, "Anything else?"

"No. That's all I have. I'll be on the island for a few more weeks. Let me know if you have any more questions for me."

They shook hands, and Heath exited the office and strode toward the station's lobby. He caught his breath at the sight of Willow still seated on one of the hard chairs in the front.

She looked up from her phone. "That was fast."

"Guess Sheriff Chandler wasn't as interested in my alibi as you thought he should be."

She bustled out of the station, and he followed her.

As they stood outside beneath the emerging sun, he dangled his flannel from his fingers. "Doesn't look like I'll need this after all."

"Before I go anywhere with you—" she snatched the shirt from his hand "—I need to have a look at this flannel."

He didn't even try to hide the surprise from his face

this time. His mouth dropped open as she examined his shirt. "What are you doing?"

"I'll tell you over breakfast. You're driving." She tossed the shirt at him, and he caught it in one hand.

As he settled behind the wheel, he asked, "Where to? It's been a while for me. Some things look different."

"Yeah, and we want to stop that from happening to the other side of the island." She tapped on the glass. "Let's go to the Harbor Restaurant. It's close, just up the hill, and they have a good breakfast."

If the DFSD had a good view, the Harbor Restaurant and Bar had a better one. Floor-to-ceiling windows looked over Discovery Bay and Dead Falls Island's harbor.

He'd left his flannel shirt in the car. He didn't know what Willow expected to find in it, but he didn't want to trigger her.

After the hostess seated them by a window and the busboy dropped off a couple of waters, Heath planted his elbows on the table. "Do you want to tell me what's going on?"

Willow reached into her purse and pulled out a scrap of red material. She waved it over the table. "Look familiar?"

Pinching the cloth between his fingers, he tugged it from her grasp. "Looks like a piece of red flannel, but it's not from my shirt. This one has like a yellow stripe running through it. Mine has a black one."

"I figured that out. Plus, your shirt isn't missing a piece."

He took a sip of water, feeling exonerated. "You wanna tell me where you found that?"

"I found it on a branch, ringing my property." He'd

dropped the flannel on the table, and she smoothed it with her fingers. "Looks clean, doesn't it? I don't think it had been there long."

"Significance?" He flipped open the menu the waitress had dropped off and ran his finger down the breakfast items.

"Last night, before Luna ran to my place and before we discovered Toby, Apollo was whining about something in the woods outside my house. I forgot about it until I got back. So, this morning, I went to the general area where he was alerting, and I found this." She dragged the piece of cloth across the table toward her with one finger.

"You think someone was watching you?" He closed the menu and folded his hands on top of it.

"Maybe. Apollo usually barks when there's another animal. He saves his whines for humans, and he was definitely whining."

Heath picked up the piece of flannel and folded it in two. "Did you tell Sheriff Chandler about this?"

"No." She snatched the material from his fingers and shoved it into her pocket. "I wanted to check with you first."

"When you saw me with my red flannel shirt today, you figured I was the one skulking around your property?"

Two red spots formed on her cheeks. "It was a coincidence, don't you think?"

Cranking his head from side to side, he said, "Almost every person in here is wearing or carrying a flannel shirt, and red is a popular color."

"But I don't know anyone in here who was also at Toby's cabin last night." She shifted her attention from him to the waitress approaching their table. "Good morning. I'll have the avocado toast and a cup of hot tea—herbal, if you have it."

The waitress reeled off several herbal teas, took Willow's order and turned to him. "What would you like?"

"Banana pancakes, bacon on the side and some coffee." He turned his coffee mug upright on the table as the waitress walked away. Seemed like he wasn't the only one keeping secrets from the sheriff. "Why didn't you tell the sheriff?"

"I told you. I wanted to ask you about it first." Avoiding his gaze, she took her time tapping her straw on the table and peeling the paper away from it before plunging it into her glass of ice water.

He narrowed his eyes. "You really thought it was me out there and wanted to trap me before I could ditch the flannel."

"Trap you?" Her lips puckered around the straw as she took a sip of water. "I'm not Nancy Drew. I just wanted to see first if you had a chunk of material missing from your shirt. I could already see before you went in to talk to the sheriff…West…that your shirt looked intact."

"But you invited me to breakfast just to make sure." He thanked the waitress as she filled his coffee cup and set down Willow's hot water.

"I invited you to breakfast to…" She lifted one shoulder. "Not sure why. Maybe just to discuss what we saw last night. See if we're on the same page. Did West give you any indications which way the investigation was going?"

"Nope." He tipped some cream into his coffee. "Tight-lipped. So, you said Luna's okay?"

"A little nervous. She looks to the forest and whines

but hasn't tried to go back home yet." Willow stirred her ice with the straw, clinking it against the glass. "What did you see last night? I never asked you. You seemed to be there before me because you came from the back of Toby's cabin."

The food's arrival saved him from the quick retort on his lips. She seemed determined to suspect him of something. He took his time slathering butter on his pancakes and pouring a little pool of syrup on his plate.

Willow pointed her knife at his plate. "You missed a spot."

He smeared a thin glaze of butter over the very edges of the top pancake and sliced through a corner of the stack. Then he swept the pancakes through the syrup and held the impending bite over his plate, watching golden beads drip onto his bacon. "What did I see when I got there? I saw you screaming and crouching over some-one on the ground while two dogs bayed into the night like a couple of mutts from the Baskervilles."

Ignoring her own food, Willow placed an elbow on the table beside her plate and wedged her chin on her palm. "I meant prior to that. You were there before I was. I saw you coming from behind his cabin."

"Ah..." He dabbed his sticky mouth with a napkin. "You're assuming I ended in front of Toby's cabin when I came off the trail. You'd be wrong. That last part of the trail is confusing, maybe on purpose. I forked off in the wrong direction. I found my way to the back of Toby's cabin by following his lights through the trees. I realized my mistake and walked around to the front... and saw you."

She picked up her knife again and cut her avocado

toast in half. "I guess that makes sense. I know that part of the trail can be baffling, and yeah, Toby probably made it that way."

"Look, we're dancing around each other, giving each other the side-eye..."

"Me?" Her voice squeaked. "You're giving me the side-eye? I don't have any reason to harm Toby."

"I wouldn't say that. What if Toby told you he was ready to sell his property to Bradford and Son? You two had a heated argument." He drew a finger across his throat. "Sale canceled."

"You're ridiculous." She bared her teeth and took a bite of her toast.

He didn't believe for one minute that Willow Sands could harm a flea on Apollo's back, but if she suspected him of killing Toby, he wanted her to know what it felt like.

"What I was trying to say is that maybe we're getting worked up for nothing. Chandler's the new sheriff in town. He probably just wants to get this right. Toby's death could be an accident or natural causes. He did have health issues."

"I guess we'll find out." She dusted crumbs from her fingers onto her plate and tilted her chin at the door. "They sure got here quickly."

Heath swiveled his head to the side, his gaze landing on a couple by the hostess stand, the chic woman pointing to a table by the window and the man, overdressed for the island, burying his face in his phone.

"Who are they?" he asked.

While Willow flapped a hand in front of her mouth, indicating she was still chewing, Heath watched the couple as the woman, her eyes wide, jabbed the man in the arm with her elbow. Her companion followed her pointing finger and bobbled his phone as he zeroed in on Heath and Willow. With two spots of color high on her cheeks, the woman grabbed the man's arm and marched toward their table, bumping a chair and causing a waiter to zigzag out of her way.

Heath tapped the handle of his knife on the table in front of Willow. "Incoming."

Willow glanced up from her dangling tea bag and whispered, "What the heck?"

The woman landed next to their table, her chest heaving, her dark eyes flashing. "There you are, you conniving witch."

Chapter Five

Willow's hand jerked, and her tea sloshed over the rim of her cup, flicking hot droplets of liquid on her knuckles. "What? Excuse me?"

"Hey. Back off." Heath sat forward in his seat, holding up a hand in Ellie Keel's direction.

Willow didn't need his protection from Ellie or her brother, but his gesture caused a warm glow in her belly.

Garrett shuffled his feet beside his sister, as his gaze took a quick inventory of Willow from hair to chest. "Hello there, Willow, all grown up."

Dabbing her hand with a napkin, Willow swallowed. Ignoring Garrett's leer, she said, "I don't know what you're talking about, Ellie. I'm sorry for your uncle's death, but he was already dead when I found him. There's nothing I could've done to help him."

"This is Ellie and Garrett Keel?" Heath's eyes narrowed as he took in the fuming woman beside their table and her slick brother next to her.

"Wait a minute." Ellie jabbed a finger, topped with scarlet nail polish the same shade as her sneering lips, in Heath's face. "You're Heath Bradford of Bradford and Son. What is going on here?"

Willow raised her eyebrows at Heath as they exchanged a glance. "Why don't *you* tell *us*? You're the one who came charging up here, interrupting our breakfast."

"Business meeting?" Ellie tapped a nail on the table as the waitress squeezed past her to raise the coffeepot at Heath.

"More coffee?"

Heath shook his head. "No, thanks."

"Hon?" Ellie grabbed the waitress's upper arm with her talons and nodded toward a window table two down from theirs. "Can you make sure we get two coffees and waters at that table?"

The waitress glanced at the hand clawing her arm and rolled her eyes. "Sure, *hon*."

Tipping a little more hot water from the mini teapot on the table into her cup, Willow said, "This is not a business meeting, Ellie. I don't know why you're upset with me. I'm sure your uncle's death was a shock…"

Ellie's nostrils flared. "Don't be coy, Willow. You must've known about Uncle Toby's will. Hell, you probably helped him write it."

"Your uncle's will?" Willow tilted her head. Ellie's statements were getting more and more bizarre. "Again, I don't have a clue what you're talking about. Toby died yesterday, and you're already checking his will?"

"We've been suspicious for a while, so of course we wanted to confirm things with his attorney this morning on our way out to the island." She smacked the table with the flat of her hand. "Suspicions confirmed."

"Still don't know what you're talking about, Ellie." Willow shook her head and took a calming sip of tea.

"Why so much drama, Ellie? Spit it out." Garrett stuffed

his phone in his pocket. "Uncle Toby left his land to you, Willow. All of it."

Willow choked on her tea and clicked the cup back in its saucer. "You're not serious."

"Deadly, as it turns out." Ellie wagged her finger between Willow and Heath. "You two already working out some deal? The laugh's on Uncle Toby, huh? I'm sure you coerced him into leaving the property to you once you assured him you'd protect it against all the mean developers."

Willow's mouth hung open until she stole a glance at Heath, who looked equally surprised. And suspicious? Did he believe Ellie that she knew about Toby's will? She snapped her mouth shut.

"I didn't know anything about your uncle's will, Ellie. He and I never discussed his business, although he probably figured I wouldn't be as eager to sell off the property as you and your brother." Willow deliberately picked up her phone and stared at it. "Imagine that. Toby hasn't even been dead for twenty-four hours, and you already know what's in his will."

Ellie sniffed. "Some of us weren't privy to it in advance."

"Okay, that's enough." Heath sliced his hand through the air, as if to dissipate the tension and anger. "You'd better go claim your table before someone else takes it."

"We're not done here, Tree Girl. We plan to fight this." Ellie spun around, crooking her finger at Garrett.

Garrett winked at Willow before joining his sister.

"Wow. What a surprise. I don't blame Ellie for being angry, but it's not like she or Garrett ever visited Toby or spent much time with him." Willow stuffed a bite of avocado toast in her mouth, the crunching from her chewing reverberating like falling boulders in the silence.

As she swallowed, she watched Heath break off a piece of bacon and crumble it in his fingers.

She dropped her toast onto her plate. "What? What are you thinking?"

"Like you said, it's a surprise." He blotted his greasy fingers with a napkin. "It just…changes a lot."

"Before you ask—" she held up a hand "—I'm not interested in selling the property to Bradford and Son. I mean, if Ellie's challenge to the will fails. If it's successful, I guess you'll have to take it up with them."

His whiskey-colored eyes picked up the light from the window and practically glowed as he studied her face. "Did you really not know about Toby Keel's will?"

"I didn't look shocked to you? I'm not that great of an actress." She circled a finger in the air, encompassing Heath's suspicious face and questioning gaze, a sticky patch of syrup on his lip. "You don't believe me. You think I sweet-talked Toby into leaving that property to me, and then what? I killed him to make sure I get my hands on it, all to protect it from greedy developers like you and the casino expansion?"

He snorted. "Of course not. I don't believe for one minute you'd harm Toby…or anyone else. Although the way you're drilling me with those stormy green eyes of yours right now, I might be inclined to hire protection."

She dropped her gaze to the mangled toast on her plate. He might've misinterpreted the look in her eyes. She did have an inclination to devour him, but not out of anger. Sighing, she shoved her plate away and curled a finger around the handle of her teacup. "I don't know what Toby was thinking. I hope Ellie and Garrett are mistaken, even though they'd probably sell you that land in a heartbeat."

"They're both older than I expected. Harder to handle, I imagine."

"They are the children of Toby's older brother. There's probably less than fifteen years' age difference between them. Toby wasn't that old, just in poor health."

Heath steepled his fingers. "If they do launch a lawsuit, you wouldn't fight it?"

"Oh, sure I would, but that fight might be better than being the landholder and reviled on all sides." She swirled her tea before taking a sip of the lukewarm brew. "I suppose I'd better find out who Toby's attorney was and make a call."

"You might want to tell Sheriff Chandler about this development before the damning duo does their damage— unless they've already told him." Heath signaled to the waitress with a raised finger.

"You're probably right. If I'm the new owner of that property, I'd rather be the one to give West the news." She reached for the check the waitress slid onto the table. "Do you really think the sheriff is going to see that as a motive for me to kill Toby?"

He snatched the bill from her hand. "We don't even know yet if anyone killed Toby, but I'm sure the sheriff will perform his due diligence. Seems like an okay guy, unlike some of the other sheriffs we've had on the island."

"You say that as if you're a local." Willow pulled a ten and a five from her purse and shoved them at Heath. She couldn't have him thinking he could buy her off. "You weren't here that long, as I remember it."

"I lived here for a few years as a teenager. That was when my parents were trying to work things out. My mother grew up on Dead Falls Island, and when she… got sick, she wanted to return to her childhood home. My father, in typical Brad Bradford fashion, bought her a huge house in a new development, thinking that would satisfy her."

"I take it the house didn't work."

Heath blinked and swept up her money while replacing it with plastic. "Didn't work."

As Willow gathered her purse in her lap, she felt her phone buzzing in the side pocket. Wrinkling her nose, she studied the unfamiliar Seattle number. "I'd better answer this, given the circumstances." She spoke quietly into the phone. "Hello?"

"Is this Willow Sands?"

"It is."

"Glad I reached you. This is Jason Hart, Toby Keel's attorney."

Willow clutched the phone as she watched Heath sign the check and pocket his credit card. "I was actually going to call you once I found your number."

"Oh? Did Toby already inform you of his plans?"

"No. I had no idea what was in his will. We never discussed it, but I was attacked by Ellie and Garrett Keel this morning, accusing me of all kinds of things."

He cleared his throat. "That's why I wanted to contact you so quickly. I gave them the bad news this morning after they called and gave me the worse news about Toby. Didn't think they'd track you down so fast."

"They were speedy."

"I have some papers for you to sign, Ms. Sands, but

I'll come to you. I have plans to head out to the island anyway. Can we meet when I get there?"

"Of course. Call me when you arrive, and we'll set up something. Just so you know, I didn't discuss Toby's land with him at all."

"Oh, I know that. He had some arrangement with your father. He bought the land from him, right?"

"Yeah." Willow wrinkled her nose and shrugged at Heath, watching her closely. "I was unaware of any kind of arrangement with my dad."

"I'll tell you about it when I get to the island."

"Okay, Mr. Hart. Thanks for the call."

"Call me Jason, and I'll see you in a few days."

Willow ended the call and tapped the edge of the phone against her chin. "That was weird."

"Toby's attorney?"

"Jason Hart. He told me Toby and my dad had some kind of arrangement."

"Regarding the land?"

"You know, my dad sold it to him originally."

"I don't remember that, but it makes sense that he left it to you, then. Maybe that was the agreement."

She scooted back from her chair, suddenly anxious to get away from all the turmoil. "My father never told me about it."

Heath put a hand on her back as they passed the table where Ellie and Garrett were sitting, both on their phones and oblivious to everything around them. His firm hand steered her toward the entrance as if protecting her against a couple of wild bears.

Once in his car, he turned to her. "Are you going to

tell the sheriff about the will when I take you back to the station?"

"The sooner, the better." She snapped her seat belt. "Where does that leave you?"

"Soundly on this island. I still have some business to conduct." He winked at her. "And don't discount my powers of persuasion so easily."

Shifting in her seat, she stared out the window. When a simple wink from Heath Bradford's eye sent flutters to all the right parts of her body, she had no doubts at all about his powers.

He pulled up to the station, his engine idling. "Do you want me to go in with you? I can at least be a witness to the Keels' animosity toward you."

"That's okay. I'm sure Ellie's animosity will come out when she sues me for that land." She slid from the truck, and resting a hand on the door, she said, "Thanks for the ride and the verification that you weren't lurking in the woods outside my cabin."

"Glad I could clear myself, but if I wasn't the one in the woods, who was?"

She shrugged and slammed his door. As she meandered toward the entrance to the sheriff's station, she fingered the soft piece of cloth in her pocket. She couldn't run around and invite every man…or woman…with a red flannel shirt to breakfast to interrogate them.

Her visit to the station didn't last long, as Sheriff Chandler was out. Nobody else could or would give her any information about the investigation into Toby's death.

She'd lost a morning's work, so she headed straight back to her cabin. She'd left the dogs on a couple of long leads—long enough to reach their water and beds outside, but short enough to keep them out of the woods. She didn't want Luna snuffling around Toby's cabin.

As she drove up to her place, she hunched over the steering wheel to look for the dogs. Apollo knew enough to not run toward her truck, but Luna was probably still feeling displaced and anxious.

She eased back when she spotted them both asleep near the firepit. As she parked and swung open her door, she braced for Apollo's assault. He always hobbled over to greet her.

Her heart jumped when she shut the truck door and still neither of the two dogs stirred from their nap.

"Apollo! Luna!"

Dropping her bag, she rushed toward the dogs lying on their sides, the ropes still attached to their collars. Had tying them up left them as prey for some forest predator?

She crouched beside them and sucked in a sharp breath as she wiped bubbles of foam from Apollo's mouth. She placed her hand on his barrel chest and gave a sob when she felt the gentle rise and fall of his breathing.

She crawled to Luna, who whimpered in her sleep when Willow touched her face. Prodding the dog did nothing to rouse her. She ran her hands along Luna's fur, much like she did last night, but didn't feel any wound or even see any blood this time.

Willow sat back on her heels and surveyed the ground around the two sleeping dogs. No signs of a fight or scuffle or animal attack. Her gaze tripped over a lump of something organic a few feet from Apollo, and she lunged toward it.

She grabbed the bloody piece of meat in her hand

and squeezed it through her fingers. A blue pill oozed out of the mass.

On her hands and knees, she searched the rest of the yard for any vestiges of the drugged lures. She scooped up a few intact balls of meat with the same blue pills embedded in the middle.

She rose to her feet, shock making her movement and thoughts lethargic. Someone had come onto her property and drugged the dogs. Why? Her gaze floated from the tree line to her truck to the firepit to the dogs and then finally to her porch, littered with splintered wood.

The mess on her porch gave her a shot of adrenaline, and she darted toward her cabin. Kicking aside the wood, she pushed open her damaged front door.

As she stood on the threshold, she gaped at the upheaval before her. Someone had ransacked her place.

Chapter Six

"The Samish call this 'where the mist meets the earth'?" Heath's gaze dropped to the white tendrils circling the ground, the swirl of it almost hypnotizing.

His Realtor, Astrid Mitchell, cleared her throat. "This particular area is called Misty Hollow. I think you'll find that Samish description applies to many locales on the island. What do you think?"

Heath thought he'd like to start digging right now. "I like the location. The aspect is great. I know a two-story house won't give me a view of the falls, but it wouldn't be half bad."

"So, you're thinking residential instead of commercial property, right? You can go commercial here, but that means pulling a few strings with the zoning commission." Astrid cupped a hand over her sunglasses and stood on her tiptoes. "We have a visitor."

"Not competition for the property, I hope." Heath turned toward the oncoming SUV plowing through the mist.

"Nope, Sheriff Chandler just bought another property on the island." She waved as the sheriff pulled up.

He stepped out of his vehicle. "Sorry to interrupt, babe,

but I was in the area and I knew you were showing out here. Hey, Heath."

Heath let out a breath. These two must be in a relationship, and that was how the sheriff had known about his interest in the Misty Hollow site. "Sheriff. Good to see you again. Anything new on Keel's death?"

"Nothing yet, and call me West. Sorry to barge in. I'm taking my girl to lunch, but you two carry on. I can wait."

Her face now beaming, Astrid turned to Heath. "Is there anything else I can show you, Heath? Once you get past the property's ghoulish history, it's a great location."

Heath turned in a slow circle, taking in the land and the ramshackle ranch house. Did this property hold even more ghoulish history than the family massacre that had taken place twenty years ago? Were other secrets buried here? Would those secrets be buried with Toby Keel?

"I'm good, Astrid. If you don't mind leaving me behind to wander by myself, I'll have another look around. You go have lunch with West." Heath held his breath as the sheriff walked past the bed of his truck, hoping he wouldn't notice or ask about the shovel and pick stowed there.

"Look around all you like and call me if you have any more questions." She hooked her arm around West's. "Where to for lunch, Sheriff? I'll follow you."

West's cell phone rang loudly, and he twisted his lips. "You might be able to stay here with Heath after all. Chandler here," he said, answering his phone.

Heath turned away as West paused on the phone. He hoped the sheriff would take Astrid away for lunch and leave him to explore the property on his own.

"Willow Sands's cabin? Again, out there? What the hell is going on? I'll be right there."

Heath spun around and said, "Is Willow okay? I just saw her for breakfast this morning."

"She's fine. Cabin was ransacked." West kissed Astrid on the forehead. "Meet you at the Grill in about an hour?"

Astrid huffed out a breath. "Of course. I hope Willow is all right."

"I'm following you over there." Heath held up his hands. "I won't interfere, but I want to check on Willow. What about the dogs?"

"My deputy didn't say anything about the dogs. You can come, but stay out of her cabin until we're done with our investigation."

"Got it." Heath thrust out his hand to Astrid. "Thanks for meeting me out here again. Any objection if I mosey out this way later and have another look?"

"None at all. I want to make this sale, Heath." She winked at him and waved at West.

Not that he needed to this time, but Heath followed West out to Willow's cabin, his thumbs drumming a beat on the steering wheel. This assault on Willow's home obviously had something to do with Toby's death. Was it some kind of warning, or was someone looking for something?

Was his father capable of threats like this? He knew his father was capable of many deeds that made Heath's continued employment and association with Bradford and Son almost untenable. Did he have the guts to follow his principles and make a move? Could he drive the old man out of his own company?

If Dead Falls Island gave up its secrets to Heath, he

might have all the ammunition he needed to oust his father from Bradford and Son.

By the time he reached Willow's property, minutes behind the sheriff, Heath had convinced himself that Bradford and Son had something to do with this recent threat against Willow. He hadn't quite persuaded himself that the company was also responsible for Toby's death, but the idea had occurred to him that someone might have discovered that Heath had been in touch with Toby for reasons other than the land deal.

One look at Willow's ashen face as she sat on the ground with Apollo's head in her lap banished every other thought in his head except the desire to protect her and make everything right. If the intruders had also killed Apollo and Luna, Willow would be devastated.

He scrambled out of his truck and rushed to Willow's side. "Are you okay?"

She nodded. "I'm fine. I got here after the fact. Didn't interrupt anyone doing the deed, but I wish I had been here."

"I'm glad you weren't." He stroked Apollo with one hand and Luna with the other as a substitute for what he really wanted to do—take Willow in his arms and hold her close. "The dogs aren't dead. What happened to them?"

She pointed to a plastic bag containing raw meat. "Someone wrapped up some pills in meat and tossed it to the dogs. I'm saving that for the vet. She's coming to look at the dogs but said as long as they're breathing steadily and not vomiting or foaming at the mouth, they'll probably be fine. They've just been in a pretty deep sleep since I discovered them."

"So someone incapacitated the dogs to get to your

cabin and what?" He pried open Luna's eye, and she stirred and whined. "West said your place was tossed."

She flicked her fingers at West talking to one of his deputies on the porch as he examined the splintered door. "Is he consulting with you now?"

He felt her barb pierce his chest. Their easy camaraderie over breakfast had ended with a busted door. "I was with Astrid Mitchell at the Misty Hollow property when the sheriff drove up. I guess the two of them are in a relationship and had a lunch date. He got the call when he was standing there, and I insisted on following him."

Her green eyes narrowed to a cat's stare. "Why?"

Shoving a hand through his hair, he said, "Chill, Willow. I wanted to make sure you were okay after what we witnessed last night. That doesn't make me a stalker or someone complicit in the break-in. Is that what you think?"

"Did you tell your daddy that I was the lucky recipient of Toby's land?"

"No." As Willow sank back next to Apollo and rubbed his head, Heath said, "But I did call the office. Of course I did. That's just business."

She shot back up, her spine erect. "Shady business. You tell your cronies at Bradford that I inherited Toby's property, and minutes later someone drugs my dogs and trashes my house."

"Exactly." He rolled his eyes in relief. She'd just vanquished any suspicions he had of the company being involved here. "*Minutes* later. Think about it. Do you really believe Bradford and Son has a goon squad on call to perpetrate violence against land holdouts?"

Leveling a finger at him, she said, "*You* think about it.

If that goon squad was already in the area to take care of Toby, they wouldn't have had to go too far, would they?"

"The company doesn't have an enforcement division waiting in the wings." Even as the words left Heath's mouth, dozens of dirty tricks he'd suspected Bradford of perpetuating marched across his brain.

He tipped his head toward a white van rolling up, with the words Mobile Vet inscribed across the side in blue. "I think your vet's here to check out the dogs."

"Willow!" West gestured with his hand in the air. "We need you to check for missing items."

"You go." Heath nudged Willow's shoulder with his elbow. "I'll handle the dogs."

On her way to answer the sheriff's questions, Willow stopped to talk to the vet, who had the lowdown by the time she reached Heath and the two sleeping dogs.

"Hi, I'm Dr. Jaimie. Willow told me what happened."

"I'm Heath. If you need any help with the dogs, let me know. Do you think you'll be taking them into the van?"

"From what Willow told me and the looks of these two, I don't think so." Dr. Jaimie reached over and opened the plastic bag with the meat. Running her thumb across one of the blue pills, she squinted at it. "This is a tranquilizer, not poison. Even if the dogs ate several of these, it won't kill them. Whoever did this wanted to knock out a couple of guard dogs, and that's what they got."

"Just a long nap."

"Pretty much."

The vet grasped the stethoscope around her neck and proceeded to check the vitals of each animal. Luna stirred several times and whimpered in her sleep. Even Apollo snorted a few times as the doc prodded him.

Heath glanced over Dr. Jaimie's head as Willow exited her cabin, her face set in a scowl. *Must be bad in there.*

She and West approached the vet together, and Jaimie turned her head to greet the sheriff. "How's Sherlock doing, West?"

"He's doing great. Follows Olly around everywhere." West explained to Heath. "Olly is Astrid's son, and Sherlock is a stray they adopted."

Dr. Jaimie ran her hand through the fur of a still-groggy Apollo. "I hope nobody is running around the island drugging pets."

"I think that's reserved for my pets." Willow crouched beside the vet. "Are they okay? Will they need any treatment?"

"Their vitals are strong. Luna is already showing signs of coming around, probably because she's younger than Apollo, but he's doing okay. They just need to sleep it off." With two fingers, the vet picked up the plastic bag with the meat and dangled it in the air. "Is it okay if I take this, West? I can tell by the markings on the pill that it's a tranquilizer, but I'd like to test it."

"Unless there's another one, I'm going to have to take it for evidence."

"There was another one." Willow jerked her thumb over her shoulder. "I gave it to Deputy Fletcher when he first showed up."

"Then keep it, Jaimie." West squeezed Willow's shoulder. "I think you should invest in a security system, Willow."

Willow pulled her bottom lip between her teeth. "I can't even get Wi-Fi out here."

Heath said, "There are still security cameras that record directly to a hard drive. You don't need Wi-Fi. I can handle that for you."

"I think I can figure that out myself." Willow jumped to her feet, dusting the knees of her jeans.

As she and the vet talked, Heath edged closer to West. "Was anything taken from her cabin?"

"Not that she could tell. Computer, guns, a few expensive jewelry items—all safe." Hooking a thumb in his belt loop and tilting his head back, West surveyed the remote property. "You should encourage her to get a camera up sooner rather than later."

"As if I have any pull with her." Heath spread his arms. "She has the idea that Bradford and Son is responsible for this."

"There is some high-stakes land grabbing out here, isn't there?" West raised an eyebrow in his direction. "Are you sure your company *isn't* involved?"

Heath let that go. At least the sheriff wasn't accusing Bradford and Son of murder...yet.

Dr. Jaimie and Sheriff Chandler wrapped up at the same time, and pulled away from Willow's property one right after the other, leaving Heath alone with Willow, crouching over the dogs.

"Let me at least get the mutts comfortable." Before she could protest his help, Heath scooped up Apollo and carried him to a bed near the cabin's porch. He followed suit with Luna, placing her down gently on the sheepskin. "They'll probably be thirsty when they wake up."

"At least they're going to wake up." She pushed open her damaged door, and Heath peeked inside the cabin, his eyes widening.

"They did a number on your place. Do you need help cleaning up?"

Wedging a hand on her hip, she looked him up and down. "First the security camera, now the cabin cleanup. Do you feel guilty or something?"

"I just wanna help." He crossed his arms over his chest. "And I'm going to start with that door. You need to get it fixed before night falls. Is Gem Hardware still in town, or are you going to have to get a door from the mainland?"

"Gem is still there." Her tense shoulders finally dropped. "Why are you so invested in helping me?"

"I don't see anyone else stepping up."

"You're assuming I can't handle cleaning up and getting the repairs done myself."

"Why should you do it alone?" He squeezed past her and inspected the doorjamb. "Someone kicked this in or used some kind of battering ram to break it apart."

"That's what West figured." She waved a hand behind her at the disheveled cabin. "I don't think they were looking for anything, or at least, I can't imagine what they hoped to find. I believe this is just an intimidation tactic—sell the land or else."

"There are several interested parties here, not just Bradford and Son." He held up a hand and ticked off his fingers. "Ellie and Garrett are mad enough to take some kind of action. Then there's the Samish. It's in their best interest for Bradford to develop this land for the casino."

"The Samish are going to build that casino with or without the adjacent land."

"True, but they'll realize bigger profits from the casino if Bradford can add some hotels, restaurants and infrastructure to support it." He stepped into the room and plucked up a throw pillow. "I'll start with the easy stuff."

He darted around the room, stuffing cushions back onto sofas and chairs, righting tables and stacking papers. He picked up a few books pulled from a shelf and slotted them back in place. Several framed pictures on the shelf had been knocked down, and he studied one photo as he turned it over.

Tapping the unbroken glass on the frame, he asked, "Is this your mother?"

"Yeah, before she took off for greener pastures." Hugging a pillow to her chest, Willow stood on her tiptoes and peeked over his arm.

"D-did she disappear, or do you know where she is? Have you had contact with her since she left?"

Willow dropped down to her heels, barely reaching his shoulder. "Of course I know where she is…or mostly. She's in Central America right now. Costa Rica, I believe. I'll have to check her blog to find out for sure."

"Your mother has a blog?"

"A vlog, actually. A travel vlog for single women of a certain age." She tossed the pillow onto a love seat. "It's quite popular, actually. She even earns enough to support herself."

"Good for her, I guess. Not so much for you."

Pushing her hair back, Willow made a sad face. "It hurt when I was little. Now? Not so much. Your mom left when you were older, right? When you were living on Dead Falls."

"That's right, but the difference is I never heard from her again. She disappeared."

Willow's mouth dropped open. "What do you mean, disappeared?"

"Exactly that. She left one day, leaving a note for us, and we never heard from her again. At least, I didn't."

"Did your father?"

"I don't know. He won't talk about it, but a few years ago after no contact, he had her declared dead." Heath choked on the words and coughed to hide it.

"That's…that's terrible." She rested her hand on his back with a featherlight touch. "What did the note say?"

"It said she was going to end her life."

"Heath, no." She covered her mouth. "Do you think she was serious?"

"My mom suffered from depression. She'd been in therapy, had medication, but nothing seemed to work. My dad thought being back on Dead Falls would help. It didn't."

"But suicide." Willow's eyes shimmered with tears. "Her body was never found? Did she leave the island?"

"The sheriff at the time conducted a cursory investigation. A ticket purchased shows she took a ferry back to the mainland, but she'd left her phone at home. Her purse and credit cards were gone, but she never used them."

"I'm so sorry. I had no idea at the time. I guess I'd heard that your mom left, but I didn't know the details."

He rubbed a hand across his mouth. He hadn't meant to get into this with her. "Nobody did. My dad kept things pretty quiet."

"I thought losing a mom the way I did was bad, but at least I can visit her vlog to check on her." She patted his back awkwardly. "If you want to pick up that door at Gem Hardware, I'll give you my debit card, and you can knock yourself out. Hell, if they have a home security camera there—the low-tech kind—you can pick up one of those while you're at it."

A smile stretched his lips. "Do you think I told you that sad story so you'd let me help you?"

"I don't know, but it worked." She snatched the frame from his hand and adjusted it on the shelf.

HEATH SPENT THE afternoon making Willow feel better—or at least more secure. While she finished putting her place back together, he drove into town and purchased a replacement door, which he loaded into the back of his truck, and a security camera that fed to a hard drive.

When he got back to her place, the dogs were stirring. She helped him hang the new door and install the camera above it. She insisted on treating him to pizza from Luigi's for dinner to reward his efforts. It almost felt like a date, and his pity party had softened her stance toward him—not that he intended that result.

He hadn't meant to spill his guts at all about his mother. All anyone knew around these parts, if they remembered at all, was that his mother disappeared in the fall and never returned. His father sold the house on Dead Falls Island a few years later, but Heath never forgot it.

Apparently, Toby Keel had never forgotten it, either.

Heath collected their plates and brought them to the kitchen. "Thanks again for the pizza."

"Thanks for everything else." She joined him at the sink and held up his half-full wineglass, the red liquid catching the light and reflecting it in her eyes. "You sure you don't want to finish this off?"

"I have some work to do tonight in my hotel room, and I need a clear head for the numbers."

"I have my new door, new locks, new camera, refreshed dogs, and I don't need a clear head for anything." She tipped his glass back and gulped the rest of the wine.

He laughed. "Don't get too tipsy to handle that rifle."

"I'd probably need a few more glasses to actually shoot someone coming through the door."

"Just remember what they did to Apollo and Luna." He flicked the empty glass with his fingernail.

"You're right." She growled. "Bring it on."

"That's better." He loaded the last of the dishes in the dishwasher. "You have my number now. If you need anything, don't hesitate to call me."

She stood with her back to the counter, her hands loosely clasped in front of her, her lush lips stained with red wine. "Are you doing all this to get my property?"

The hell with the property. He had completely different motives now. He dragged his gaze away from her pout. "Told you I could be persuasive."

She showed him to the door, and he paused on the porch. "Be careful, and I mean that. Call me for anything."

Saluting, she said, "You got it, Bradford."

He cuffed Apollo's ear and loped toward his truck. As he backed up, he waved out the window. He left it open for his drive and inhaled the fresh air. He needed to clear his mind for the business at hand.

The drive to the other side of the island took longer in the dark, but he didn't want to get pulled over for speeding. Not that carrying a pick and shovel were illegal or even suspicious on Dead Falls Island, but he didn't want to draw attention to himself or his mission.

He flicked on his wipers as he crossed the bridge, the falls to his right sprinkling his windshield. Then he made the hard turn left to Misty Hollow and the cursed property.

He pulled his truck into position, facing the two big-leaf maples, and left his headlights beaming into the dark. He thumbed on the dome light and pulled the scrap of paper from his pocket, its edges soft and worn. He held it under the light and read the words aloud for the hundredth time. "'You'll find your mother where the mist meets the earth, between the giant maples.'"

The mist met the earth here, and two huge maple trees towered in front of him. Even though Toby Keel hadn't lived long enough to verify his riddle, Heath felt confident he'd found his mother's resting place.

He jumped from the truck and peeled back the tarp he'd bought at Gem Hardware today to reveal his tools. He hoisted the shovel and pick from the truck bed and strode toward the space between the two trees.

Then he plowed the shovel into the ground and started digging.

Chapter Seven

The following morning, Willow sprang out of bed to check the video footage from the night before. She scanned through the recording, noting the night critters that darted in and out of view and the mist that rolled across the ground. Nothing human crept up to her cabin.

Sighing, she slumped in her chair. Anyone could spot the camera above her porch, so it might work more as a deterrent than a spy.

Luna called her to the front door with a scratch, and she pushed up to her feet to rescue the dog.

Willow stood on the front porch, her toes curled over the edge of the top step, as she watched the dogs go about their business. They didn't seem any worse for wear after their ordeal yesterday. Who ran around drugging dogs?

She glanced over her shoulder into her cabin. The intruders must've been trying to spook her with their break-in. As far as she could tell, they'd taken nothing of value. Their tactic didn't make much sense to her, though. A few thugs ransacking her summer house were not going to suddenly convince her to sell her land... or Toby's.

Had they been looking for something else? When Dad

died and she'd come back here that first summer after her freshman year in college, she'd cleaned out a lot of his items—but not everything. Maybe his papers contained something of value that she'd missed.

Dad's family, the Sandses, did have a lot of wealth and property at some point. Mom had told her that Dad had sold it all off except this plot and the one he eventually sold to Toby. But Mom didn't always know all of Paul Sands's business.

Dad's will had kept things simple. He'd left all his worldly possessions to Willow, and he'd already put her on the title for this property, so there was no paperwork to go through at the time of his death, except to remove his name from the title. He didn't have stacks of cash or stocks or Swiss bank accounts—as far as she knew.

But maybe someone knew something she didn't.

Rubbing the back of her neck, she strolled into the house. She'd have to dig out Dad's old stuff to see if she could find something. The trespassers had gone through some papers, as they'd strewn the evidence across her floor, but they probably hadn't gone through the old suitcase where she'd stashed most of her father's paperwork.

She filled the dogs' bowls with food and refreshed the water in the tub outside. Then she made herself a smoothie for breakfast and carried it to the small bedroom. The cabin had only two bedrooms—the large one, which she'd taken over from her father after his death, and the smaller one, which had been her room growing up.

She placed her breakfast drink on the white nightstand with flowers painted on the drawer and sat crosslegged on the floor beside the double bed covered with a yellow comforter. The invaders had tossed this room, too, but mostly for show. They'd rifled the bookshelf, knocking over a few vampire books from her teen years, and had pulled a couple of items, mostly sports gear, from the closet.

Flipping up the comforter, she felt beneath the bed until her fingers found the handle of the battered suitcase that had belonged to her father. She curled her fingers around it and dragged the bag from under the bed.

She'd never put a lock on the suitcase but figured it had been a step up from the cardboard box where she'd found most of her father's business. He'd left the only important paper, his will, in a kitchen drawer, and had made sure she knew where to find it. She'd grabbed handfuls of this other irrelevant paperwork and shoveled it from the box into this brown suitcase.

Flipping the suitcase open now, she studied the paperwork scattered in the bottom. Did it seem like there were fewer papers in here? She wouldn't have a clue. She'd tossed these items in here, helter-skelter, figuring if someone asked for something important later, she could go through it at that time. Nobody ever had. She grabbed a piece on top, scanning a letter about brush clearance from the Forest Service. How would she know if someone had gone through this mess?

Dropping the Forest Service letter on the floor, she noticed her dirty fingerprints on the page. She hadn't dragged this suitcase from its hiding place for years, and it was dusty. If someone else had been here before her, there should be more fingerprints.

To avoid leaving more prints, she grabbed the shredded silky lining inside the lid of the bag and tugged it down, removing her fingers at the last second when it closed. A few eddies of dust floated upward with the closure, caught in the rays of sun from the window, but not a lot.

She squinted at the top of the suitcase, making out her fingerprints on the edge of the lid, left when she'd opened the bag. But her marks in the dust weren't the only ones there. Larger swaths of dust had been removed, as if other prints were left in the general area of hers, but then wiped out with a sleeve or a cloth. Or perhaps the thief had worn gloves and had cleared the dust off with his hands.

Her nose tingled with the release of the dust in the air, and she rubbed it with the back of her hand. "Well, I'll be damned."

The intruders had found this case and opened it. Whether or not they'd taken anything would have to remain a mystery, as Willow had no idea what she'd shoved in there.

Should she tell West? She played out that absurd conversation in her head and rejected it. The strangers, in the course of going through her cabin, had also looked into this suitcase, but she didn't know what had been in it or if anything was now missing. She pushed the case back under the bed and wiped her hands on her pajama bottoms.

The dogs started barking out front, and the growl of an engine carried into the cabin. Willow grabbed her smoothie and scurried to the front door, which she'd left wide open.

When she spied Heath getting out of his truck, her heart still beat furiously, but in a different kind of pattern. It seemed as if they'd just parted company hours ago, and here he was again. He either really wanted to see her, or he wanted to keep applying some subtle pressure on her.

She plucked at her flannel pajama bottoms but took some pleasure in the fact that his hair stood on end and he needed a shave. She could put down her own appearance to a couple of glasses of wine the night before, but he'd pretty much abstained. What was his excuse for his tired appearance?

Cupping a hand over her eyes, she said, "What brings you out here so early? I'm still not selling."

"Early?" He rubbed the top of Apollo's head. "It's almost eleven o'clock."

The dogs had barked at the arrival of his truck, but he'd already earned their trust and devotion. Once they saw Heath get out of the truck, they'd stopped barking.

"Is it?" She took a sip of her drink and caught a drop of the thick smoothie at the corner of her mouth with her tongue. "I swear, I haven't gotten any work done out here."

"What's been going on hasn't exactly been conducive to cataloging flora and fauna." He made a circling motion in the air. "Everything go okay with the camera setup?"

"I looked at the footage this morning, and except for a skunk drinking from the dogs' water dish, nothing much happened."

"That's good to hear. Just wanted to make sure the security system was in working order. It'll at least function as a deterrent." Heath clapped a hand over his mouth and yawned.

"You must've had a lot of work last night."

Dropping his hand, Heath jerked his head up. "Why do you say that?"

"Um, because you told me you had work to do, and this morning you can barely keep your eyes open." She tipped her head toward her open door. "Would you like some coffee? I haven't made it yet. Clearly, I haven't done much of anything this morning, but it'll just take a few minutes."

"I'll take you up on that. The coffee from the hotel lobby was so vile, I couldn't stomach it." On his way to the porch, he crouched down to give Luna a hug.

Must be missing his own pooches.

Once inside, Heath sank into a chair at the kitchen table. "No leftover pizza for breakfast?"

"Leftover veggie pizza is kind of gross. You should've taken the pepperoni that was left over. I'll never eat it."

"I'll take it now." He brushed past her in the small kitchen and opened her fridge. He snatched up the plastic bag that contained the leftovers from their meal last night.

She punched the button to start the coffee brewing. "Do you want to heat that up in the microwave?"

"Negative. Better cold." To prove his point, he bit off the tip of a piece of pepperoni pizza straight from the fridge.

While Heath ate his breakfast, Willow watched the coffee drip into the pot. She poured two cups and carried them to the table. "Cream or sugar?"

"Black." He curled two fingers around the handle of the mug and lifted it. "Breakfast of champions."

Tapping next to a blister on his finger, she said, "That looks nasty."

"Yeah, well, I'm not above manual labor, as I proved yesterday. Must've gotten that while I was hanging the door." He blew on the steam wafting from his cup and took a sip. "So much better than what the hotel has to offer. Anything more from the Keels after yesterday's ambush?"

"No, but Toby's attorney, Jason Hart, called me and wants to meet this afternoon. I'm hoping he can explain what's going on." She clicked her fingernail against her mug, watching the cream swirl in the mocha-colored liquid.

"What's wrong? Feeling guilty about inheriting that property? I can assuage you of that guilt." Heath quirked his eyebrows up and down.

"N-no. I'm just coming to the realization that I didn't know much about my father's affairs."

"Why would you? You were just a teenager when he passed. You didn't get any help from the adults in your life at the time, did you?"

"My mother was in Bali at the time." She twisted her lips into a semblance of a smile.

"You're lucky, though. Other than this house and the strings attached to the property he sold Toby, sounds like your father's assets were simple and straightforward." He plopped another slice of pizza onto his plate.

"I thought so, but…"

Apollo cut off her confession with a high-pitched whine, and she scrambled from her chair. Standing at the front door, she called to Apollo, pacing in front of the tree line. "What's wrong, boy? Where's Luna?"

Heath came up behind her, cradling his coffee mug. "What's he crying for?"

"Not sure, but I don't see Luna anywhere."

"The way Apollo's stalking the edge of the forest there, I'd bet a few bucks Luna headed into the woods, probably back to Toby's."

"That's what I've been afraid of. That's why I kept her on a lead yesterday, which probably made it easier for the intruders to drug them."

"The DFSD must be done processing that scene by now. Hell, it may even just be the scene of an accident. I don't think there's any harm in Luna going there."

"Probably not, but I don't want her going through the forest. She's completely domesticated." She whistled for Apollo, and he loped to her side, head hanging. "Don't worry, Apollo. We'll bring her back."

"I'll drive you over in my truck." Heath popped the last bit of crust into his mouth and brushed his hands together. "Get dressed. I'll take care of the dishes. You see? Luna's not the only one who's domesticated."

"I thought you were a bachelor."

"Bachelors have to be even more domesticated, or we'll end up living in squalor." He nudged the small of her back. "If you want to take a shower before you get dressed, I think Luna will be fine."

"That sounds like a broad hint. I must smell like dog, wine and sweat."

"Whatever it is, I like it." He took her coffee cup from her as they entered the house and made a beeline for the kitchen.

"You are really working it, Bradford. I might just make you believe there's hope to keep the groveling coming."

He parked himself in front of the sink. "I obviously have to work on my sincerity."

She couldn't wipe the smile from her face as she traipsed into her room to gather some clothes and cranked on the shower for a quick wash. The man had charm to spare, and its effect was dizzying.

She still had no plans to sell either property to Bradford and Son, but how far would Son go to change her mind?

As HEATH RINSED the dishes, he ran a thumb over the blister on the side of his finger. His digging last night had yielded nothing...except this blister. He'd looked over the land but didn't see any other pair of maple trees together. Had Toby been messing with his mind?

Toby had been the one to contact Heath with his cryptic, unsigned notes. Heath had only figured out that Toby Keel was his anonymous pen pal by luck. When his father had told him to start securing the properties on the west side of Dead Falls Island to dovetail with the Samish casino plans, Heath had recognized Toby's handwriting from several documents.

Toby had admitted to being the author, and the two had planned to meet so that Toby could come clean about what he knew regarding the disappearance of Heath's mother. Toby's death had put an end to that. Had someone made sure that Toby would die with his secrets?

Luna's escape gave Heath an excuse to check out Toby's house. Willow owned the property now. Why shouldn't she be there, and why shouldn't he be there with her to collect Luna?

He poured himself another cup of coffee and scrolled through his phone as he waited for Willow. Now he just needed an excuse to get into Toby's house. He wanted to search through the man's things to see if he'd intended to send Heath any more clues about his mother.

Why hadn't Toby just come out and told Heath what happened and where his mother was buried? He must've had something to do with his mother's death. Maybe he knew he was dying, and his conscience forced him to come clean before his death. Only he hadn't had time.

"You seem engrossed. Playing a game on your phone?"

He lifted his head as Willow walked into the kitchen, her hair swinging in a ponytail and jeans encasing her slender legs. Tilting his phone back and forth, he said, "Reception is spotty. Can't get new mail or messages."

"That's a problem out here. Hike or drive?" She pointed to two pairs of shoes stationed at the front door—white tennis shoes and scuffed hiking boots.

"Let's walk over. You can show me where you found that piece of flannel. Did you ever tell West about that?" He dumped his coffee down the drain and chased it with a blast of water.

"I gave West a call and told him everything—about Toby's will, the anger of the Keels, and I handed over that scrap of material after the break-in yesterday." She sat down on the edge of a chair and stuffed her stock-inged feet into her boots. "I can't run around grabbing everyone with a red flannel."

"Just me, but you can grab *me* all you want." As Willow's cheeks turned pink, he shook his head. "I mean, if you ever need help or…anything."

"I'm not selling, Son."

Crouching in front of Apollo, he cupped the dog's head and touched his nose to his. "A guy can't get a break around here, dude."

"And don't try to get Apollo on your side, either. He can't be bought with cheap affection." She raised a finger. "Don't even go there."

Heath left Willow's cabin with a lighter step than when he'd arrived. He'd plastered over his fatigue and disappointment with a quick smile and a jovial attitude, just like he always did, but several minutes in Willow's company turned the cover-up into reality. She had a way of making him feel at ease. The whole island did, and he'd turned her into some kind of woodsy representative of Dead Falls.

As they tromped through the woods, Heath tried to keep his gaze on the trail in front of him instead of on Willow's pert backside in those tight jeans. He'd still want her even if she didn't own one blade of grass on this island.

She stopped suddenly, and he almost plowed into her. "Whoa."

She glanced at the hand on her hip he'd used to avoid knocking her to the ground. Then she flicked a skinny branch with her fingers. "I found the flannel material here."

Taking a step back, he surveyed the area. "No reason for anyone to be hiking this trail unless he or she was going from Toby's place to yours, right?"

She rubbed her chin. "I mean, yeah, but it's part of the National Forest. Anyone has a right to be here."

"You didn't find anything else suspicious?"

"Nope. Could've been some hiker, but I thought it was a coincidence."

"I agree, especially as someone trashed your place yesterday. They must've known you were out, known about the dogs, known they were tied up." He snapped a twig between his fingers. "Like they were watching you."

"I know." She hunched her shoulders. "Let's get to Luna."

Ten minutes later, they emerged from the tree line onto Toby's property. Yellow crime scene tape sagged between a post and the picnic bench, and Luna lay beside the firepit where they'd found Toby's body just two nights ago.

Willow dabbed the corner of her eye with the tip of her finger. "That's so sad. She's waiting for Toby to come back."

Heath crept toward the dog and hunched beside her. "It's all right, girl. You don't need to protect him anymore."

Leaning above him, Willow circled her finger in the air over a spot on the ground. "West took the rock. I imagine the medical examiner is going to determine if Toby fell on it or if someone used it to bash his head."

"West is being tight-lipped about it." Heath rose to his feet, his gaze darting toward Toby's cabin. "Do you need to get anything out of Toby's cabin for Luna?"

"I have everything I need for her—" Willow shoved her hands in her pockets and kicked at one of the stones circling the firepit "—but I might need her vaccination records."

Heath lifted his shoulders. "It's not really breaking in if he left everything to you."

She pulled her hand free from her pocket and dangled a silver key in front of him. "We don't need to break in. I have a key to the cabin, just as Toby had a key to mine."

"Even better."

Willow ordered the dogs to stay as she bobbled the key in the palm of her hand. When they reached the entrance, she slid the key home and pushed open the door.

The layout of Toby's cabin mirrored Willow's, but the resemblance ended there. While Willow had turned her space into a cozy, charming, neat forest retreat, Toby had stuffed his place full of junk. Towers of books lined one wall without the benefit of a shelf. On one crowded table, Samish relics fought for space with bits of flora from the forest.

Heath wiped his forehead with the back of his hand. If he thought he was going to find any evidence of his mother's mysterious disappearance here, he'd been grossly mistaken. He whistled through his teeth. "What a mess."

"Kind of a controlled chaos." Willow picked up a red file folder from a desk and thumbed through it. "It would take weeks to find anything in here."

Throwing her a sharp look, he said, "You mean Luna's records?"

"Yeah, yeah. Luna's records. I'll just ask Dr. Jaimie. She probably has all that." She swept several folders from the desk, including the red one, and tucked them under her arm. "Maybe Toby's attorney needs some of these papers."

Heath turned his back on her and scanned the rest of the cluttered room. It felt like he wasn't the only one compelled to search through Toby Keel's life for clues. No wonder he hadn't had to twist her arm to get in here. But he couldn't do much of a search with her hanging over his shoulder.

As they stepped out of the cabin, a chill permeated

the air, and the sun struggled to reach the ground, now swirling with mist. He glanced up as moisture caressed his face. "That was fast."

"Toby's property dips just enough to be susceptible to the moisture from the ocean that gets trapped inland. He had a name for this property when my father sold it to him. I don't remember the Samish name, which is more poetic, but he called it *where the mist meets the earth*."

Chapter Eight

Heath froze beside her, and she stumbled to a stop, nearly tripping over Apollo. "Did you forget something?"

He turned in a circle and pointed to a thatch of trees near a creek that ran through the back of the property. "Are those maple trees?"

"Yes." She grabbed Apollo's collar to prevent him from backtracking to Heath. "The two big ones are big-leaf maples. Are you having second thoughts about tearing everything down and putting up a parking lot?"

"I see them around a lot. Thought they were maples but couldn't remember. There are a couple on the Misty Hollow property, too."

"They're all over." She tilted her head toward the trail back to her place. "You ready to go, or have you decided to do a nature inventory here? If that's the case, I can put you to work."

"Yeah, let's get going. I'll take Luna with me, so she doesn't make a beeline back here. But how are you going to stop her from going back home?"

"Food, warmth, affection. I guess I have to expect she'll return here occasionally and just hope she doesn't get attacked by anything feral."

"Hey, you two."

Willow spun around at the sound of a voice, slipping the file folders inside her flannel. She swallowed as Lee Scott ambled toward them, the silver from his bolo tie glinting through the haze. As the business rep for the Samish, Lee always dressed sharply. No quick getaway, but a swift offense always trumped a back-pedaling defense.

"Hi, Lee. What brings you out here?"

"I could ask you the same." Lee nodded at Heath. "Hello, Heath. Checking out the property again now that Toby has passed?"

"I guess introductions aren't necessary." She wagged her finger between the two men. "You guys know each other?"

Heath reached forward to grab Lee's hand. "Of course we do. Similar interests."

Willow thunked her forehead with the heel of her hand, even though she knew all about their shared interests. "That's right. Lee's the one leading the charge to get a casino on the island."

"We'll get it done one way or the other, Willow, with or without your land." He pressed his thin lips into a smile.

"Is that why you're here? To drool over your prospects with Toby gone?" She tugged her shirt closed, folding her arms over the files.

Lee put his hands together. "I'm here to pay my respects. Even though Toby and I were on opposite sides of the issue, he was still a brother. And you?"

Heath jingled Luna's collar. "Came to retrieve Toby's dog. Willow is keeping her for now, but she insists on going home."

"Poor thing." Lee advanced toward Luna, who bristled and snarled at him.

"I guess she's still protective of the area." Heath smoothed his hand over the top of Luna's head.

Willow glanced between Luna and Lee, narrowing her eyes. "We'll leave you to…pay your respects in peace, Lee."

"Take care, Willow. Good to see you, Heath. We might have to schedule another meeting soon."

Willow plunged into the forest with Heath hot on her heels. When they got some distance from Toby's cabin, she hissed over her shoulder. "Did you see how Luna behaved toward Lee?"

"Like a dog defending her people and property."

"Or like a dog reacting to her owner's killer."

Heath tugged on the tail of her shirt. "Now you've pegged Lee Scott as Toby's murderer? Next, you'll be pawing through his wardrobe looking for a red flannel. He's probably not even going to get the land now."

"*He* doesn't know that, does he?" She snorted. "Do you think he would've been all nicey-nice with me back there if he knew Toby left the property to me?"

"Lee Scott is an astute businessman, not a killer."

"He's got a lot riding on that casino. He wants to maximize its profits." She flipped her ponytail over her shoulder and plowed forward.

"If we ever do have that meeting, I'll see what I can find out. But I think you'll be suspicious of anyone with connections to the land. The sooner West Chandler and the medical examiner release a manner of death, the sooner we can all move on."

She shot back, "Unless that manner of death is homicide."

When they got to her cabin, Heath helped her corral the dogs inside.

As he eyed the stack of file folders she put on the kitchen table, she moved between his line of sight and the table. She didn't want to explain to him why she wanted to look through the folders or why she'd hidden them from Lee. Bradford and Son didn't need to know everything about these properties.

"I need to get ready for my meeting with Jason Hart," she said. "Thanks for coming with me to rescue Luna."

"Anytime. I hope you get the property. I really do."

"I might be a long way from that if Ellie and Garrett challenge the will, and I'll have to stand up to the likes of Lee Scott."

"I'm sure the Keels plan to contest, which will end up keeping Lee at bay. Keep me posted." He let himself out and waved.

As soon as the door closed behind him, Willow pounced on the folders. Plopping down in a chair, she flipped open the first one.

She ran her finger down a bunch of meaningless expenses and then thumbed through the rest of the papers in the folder. More of the same. Before she could get to the next folder in the stack, she glanced at her phone and cursed softly.

She had only a few minutes to get ready for her meeting with Jason Hart. She didn't plan to dress up too much, but she could at least pluck the leaves and twigs from her hair.

Ten minutes later, dressed in a pair of blue slacks and

a white blouse, she secured the dogs in the house and jumped in her truck.

Hart had an office in Seattle but kept a small home on the coast near the harbor for frequent visits. He'd chosen the Harbor Restaurant and Bar for their afternoon meeting between the lunch and the dinner crowd, and Willow wheeled into the parking lot. She grabbed her purse from the passenger seat and slung it over her shoulder. She hadn't brought the file folders with her. She had no intention of sharing them with Hart until she had a look at them herself.

As she barreled through the door, she spotted Hart at the bar. He'd told her he'd be nursing a drink, wearing a black hat. She raised her hand in his direction, and he slid off the stool, holding up his highball glass.

"Can I get you something?" he asked her.

"Let's grab a table. I'll order something then." She took his proffered hand, his fingers damp from the glass he'd just switched to the other hand. "Good to meet you."

"Nice to meet you, too, Willow." He swirled the drink, and ice clinked against the glass. "I know it's a little early, but I'm on vacation and just took my boat over this morning."

"I don't need any explanations—as long as you're sober enough to tell me what the hell is going on with this property." She pointed to a table by the window in the half-empty restaurant. "Okay if we grab that?"

The hostess hurried over with a couple of menus. "No problem."

Once they were seated, the hostess returned with a cocktail napkin for Jason's drink. He set his glass on the napkin and reached into a satchel on the seat next to him. "I have the papers for the transfer of property with me. Please remember, I wasn't your father's attorney, just Toby's. At the time your father sold the property to Toby, his attorney sent paperwork to Toby's attorney, and that's what I have now. Toby's attorney retired, and I took over."

"My father's attorney? Wasn't her name Jordan or something like that? I dealt with her when I was a teenager, so it's been a while."

"Tabitha Jordan. Sadly, she passed away."

"Did anyone replace her? Did she work for a firm?"

Jason took a sip of his drink and raised his eyebrows at her over the rim. "The dead don't need attorneys, Willow. Once I settle Toby's estate, he won't need me, either."

Willow ordered an iced tea and a salad from the waitress, while Jason ordered another Scotch.

She chewed on her bottom lip, selecting her words before blurting out anything. "Is there any reason why someone would want to see papers on the house? I mean, if someone found another will that came after the one you have, could that cancel my ownership of the property?"

"Nothing can cancel that ownership, even if Toby made twenty wills. The paperwork your father and his attorney drew up upon the sale of the property to Toby is ironclad—at least for now. No other will can supplant it."

"Why do you say 'at least for now'?"

Jason thanked the waitress as she set his second drink in front of him. He poked at the ice in his glass with a stir stick. "Ellie and Garrett Keel are going to challenge your father's will. They've already put me on notice."

"I figured they would." She took a sip of her tea. "I'm

just wondering why my father set things up this way. If he wanted Toby to have that land, he should've sold it to him with no strings attached. At the time, he couldn't have known about the plans of the Samish and predatory developers."

Jason spread his hands. "Maybe he took a good guess."

"He sold off other plots with no such stipulations. Why this piece of land?"

"I don't have the answer to that, but if you'll excuse me, my understanding is that your father had to sell off that land to live. He wasn't working, and he owed some money to your mother for the divorce."

"You don't have to tiptoe around." She chewed on the tip of her straw. "I know better than anyone that my father had issues."

"I can't help you with the whys. I'm here to satisfy the terms of Toby's will and get this property in your name, regardless of what the Keels do down the line." Jason creased his damp cocktail napkin with his thumb. "Do you have a will?"

"Me? What? No." She pushed her place setting to the side when the waitress showed up with her salad. "I'm not married. No kids. There's really just my mom."

"You should get on that. You're a woman with two very valuable properties now. If you die intestate—" he put a hand over his heart "—God forbid, but if you do die without a will, your mother will be your beneficiary, but she'll pay some heavy taxes for the privilege."

A little chill zigzagged down her spine, and she stabbed a piece of lettuce with her fork. "I could bypass my mother and leave the property to the university or something, couldn't I?"

"Of course you can." He toyed with his drink for a few seconds before taking a sip. "And make sure everyone knows it."

The zigzag turned into a river, and Willow clenched her teeth. "Why do you say that?"

"I don't know. Just seems like everyone has some kind of interest in those properties. If you leave them under the protection of some entity, maybe that interest will die down. In the meantime, the Samish can do whatever they like with their land."

"True, but Lee Scott has made it clear that profits will be maximized with the development of the lands adjoining the casino property."

"I guess that's Lee Scott's problem, then, isn't it? Don't make it yours." Jason rattled his glass one more time before draining it of the last bit of Scotch. "Do you mind if I abandon you here to finish your salad on your own? I'll leave the paperwork, of course, so you can look it over. I'll be on the island for a few days if you have any questions, and you can return everything to me in person before I go."

"No problem. Quick question." She slid the packet of papers to her side of the table. "Will you be representing the Keels when they sue me?"

"One thing at a time." He pulled several bills from his wallet and dropped them on the table. "Lunch is on me."

When Jason left, Willow flipped through the papers while eating her salad. Her father had indeed stipulated that the property return to his daughter if both he and Toby preceded her in death. Well, that happened.

So, really, Paul Sands's agreement with Toby Keel looked more like a long-term lease than a sale, and the price reflected that. Her father had charged Toby one dollar a year for the cabin and the land.

Sighing, she pushed the papers away from her. Dad never did have a head for business, but he'd gotten what he wanted in the end. That land would remain undisturbed and immune to the development that had occurred on this side of the island. And, to be on the safe side, Willow would contact an attorney when she got back to Seattle at the end of the summer and draw up a will or living trust.

She finished her salad and ordered a refill on her iced tea, as she shoveled the files Jason left into her oversize purse. She sipped her drink and scrolled through her phone, stopping at Mom's Instagram account.

Mom's latest posts detailed several hikes in Sedona. Hopefully, she was still on this side of the world. As Willow brought up her contacts, someone rapped on her table.

Willow glanced up, her stomach sinking at the sight of Ellie Keel hovering over the booth.

Ellie's nostrils flared. "I ran into Jason Hart in the parking lot. You didn't waste any time, did you?"

"Give it a rest, Ellie." Willow massaged her temple with two fingers. "Jason called me yesterday to let me know he'd be on the island this week. He wanted to handle your uncle's business as soon as possible. Think of it this way—the sooner I take possession of the property, the sooner you can get down to the business of suing me."

Undeterred, Ellie wedged a hip against the banquette. "I also saw Lee Scott."

Willow murmured, "You've been busy."

"He said you and Heath Bradford were nosing around Toby's house."

"Did he?" Willow leaned back in her seat and folded her arms. "Seems like he was the one nosing around. We were there to retrieve Luna."

"Who?"

"Luna, Toby's dog. I can see how well acquainted you were with your uncle's life. We went to collect her and ran into Lee *paying his respects*." She huffed out a breath. "I don't think Lee ever respected Toby when he was alive."

"Lee was probably there making plans. We'd already made it clear to him that we were trying to convince Uncle Toby to sell."

"Were you pressuring Toby all this time?" Willow dug her fingernails into her biceps.

"We were discussing, not pressuring. He was family." Ellie leveled a finger at her. "Just be prepared. We're coming for you."

"Maybe you already started. Did you and Garrett break into my place yesterday?"

"Break into your place?" Ellie's face grew still and she stopped tapping her foot. "Someone broke into your cabin?"

"Drugged the two dogs and ransacked my house."

"What did they take?"

"The dogs are fine—thanks for asking." She held up her phone. "You need to leave. I was about to make a phone call."

Ellie leaned forward, and Willow could already smell the booze on her breath emanating from her parted, bright red lips. "Was anything stolen?"

"Bye." Willow wiggled her fingers in the air.

Ellie flounced off toward the bar, and the man who'd been waiting for her. After several seconds of gesturing toward Willow, Ellie perched on the bar stool and took a few gulps of her Bloody Mary.

What was it with the early drinkers on this island? Everyone was too stressed out.

Willow went back to her phone and called her mother. To her surprise, Mom picked up on the second ring. "Hello, darling."

"Hey, Mom. Saw you were in Sedona, so I thought I'd give you a try. It's not often we're in the same time zone."

"Actually, that was two days ago. I'm at the Grand Canyon today, trying to book a mule trip down to the canyon, the overnight one. It's summertime, so you must be on the island—cold, dreary place."

"It's June. The weather is great."

"Ha! The weather is never great on Dead Falls Island, Willow, unless by *great* you mean *misty, gray, cool*."

"Yeah, I get it, Mom. You hate it here and always did." Willow shook her head and swallowed some tea. "There's been some…upset here on the island this summer. Toby Keel died."

"Oh, God, Toby Keel. That's a name from the past I'd rather forget."

Her mother never had anything good to say about anyone on Dead Falls. "You knew Toby?"

"Toby made it his business to know all the women on the island—him and his creepy nephew."

Willow choked on her tea. "Toby was a womanizer?"

"Yes, runs in the family, and that's all I'm gonna say about it. How'd he die? Shot by an irate husband?"

"Mom!" Willow dabbed the liquid on her chin. "He fell and hit his head on a rock, or someone bashed his head with that rock."

Mom gasped. "I told you. It was probably some man who got fed up with Toby feeding his wife mystical Samish crap."

"Just stop. The medical examiner hasn't pinpointed manner of death yet. We're still waiting, but Sheriff Chandler is on it."

"Mark my words." Her mother crunched on something. "I heard that new sheriff is a hot commodity. Do you know him?"

"I know him, but he's already in a relationship with Astrid Mitchell."

"Hmm, you'd think that girl would've learned her lesson with cops, but I hear Chandler is the real deal."

Willow rolled her eyes. "How do you know all the Dead Falls gossip, anyway?"

"I have my sources, but they obviously dropped the ball since this is the first time I heard about Toby. What about his property? Is Garrett finally getting his hands on it?"

Her mother didn't know everything that went on here. "Yeah, about that. Dad worked out some plan that gives the property to me when Toby dies."

"Your father. He would do something like that. I wondered why he'd turn that parcel over to Toby in the first place. It's a lot more valuable than the one you're sitting on."

"No, it's not." Willow waved off the waitress bearing more iced tea. "My property is a little bigger, and the cabin is much nicer—thanks to me."

"Yeah, but Toby's property has all that other stuff. I guess it doesn't matter, as it's yours now. Makes sense why Paul would ensure it went back to you. You're just like him. You'll never do anything with that land, even though you could earn a mint from it."

Willow cocked her head. Mom was losing her. "You mean sell it for the Samish casino development."

"Casino? That's small potatoes compared to the rest of it."

"The rest of what, Mom? I have no idea what you're talking about."

She clicked her tongue. "Maybe Paul didn't trust you after all, if he didn't tell you."

"Tell me what?" Willow found herself gripping the edge of the table.

"That land—Toby's and now yours—it's full of nickel, and your father owned the mineral rights. Probably worth millions."

Willow reached for her empty glass and knocked it over. A piece of ice skittered across the table. "A-are you sure?"

"Positive. It came up in the divorce proceedings, but I couldn't touch it—not that I wanted to. Look, I'm not fond of the island, but even I didn't want to see an ugly nickel mine gouge out that side of Dead Falls."

Pinching her bottom lip with her fingers, Willow thought about the search of her cabin. Were the intruders looking for the mineral rights to Toby's property?

"Why don't I know about the mineral rights if I own the property? Toby's lawyer never mentioned anything about it." As Willow asked the question, she pulled the legal paperwork from her bag and scrambled through it.

"I don't know that much about it, but I do know that mineral rights can be held separately from the property. Maybe your father sold them off to someone else." A man's voice intruded on the conversation. "Darling, I have to go. Congrats on getting that property back, and let's meet up soon."

Her mother rang off before Willow could answer. If other people knew about the nickel vein on the land, that could explain a lot. She needed to learn more about mineral rights in general and who owned them on Toby's property—because she was pretty sure she didn't.

The waitress approached again with a pitcher of tea. "Did you want more? My shift's over in about ten minutes."

"I'm sorry to keep you. I'm done."

The waitress tipped her chin toward the window. "Looks like fire season is getting an early start."

"There's a fire?" Willow twisted her head to peer out the window. Her stomach knotted when she spied a thin trail of black smoke reaching into the sky.

"Don't worry. It's not close to us. I heard it's on the other side of the island, the less populated side."

"I know exactly where it is." Willow sprang from her seat, keeping an eye on the smoke unfurling into the mist to create a gray haze that hovered over the trees. "I live there."

Chapter Nine

Heath plunged his shovel into the ground and hit rock. The reverberation reached his shoulder. He'd need the pickax for this land. Why would someone bury his mother's body out here? Was he even looking for his mother's body? Toby Keel had talked in riddles. Maybe he didn't literally mean that Heath would find his mother here, but he'd find something.

He took a deep breath and brought the shovel down a few feet from his first attempt. It sank into the dirt easier this time, so he pulled up a shovelful of dirt and tossed it to the side. He dug down a few more feet, and then started another hole in the same area.

After about thirty minutes of work, his nostrils twitched, and he stepped back from the little mound of dirt. Had Lee Scott started a fire when he was here? Heath walked to the firepit filled with cold ash and prodded a stump of scorched wood with the toe of his boot.

When he turned in a circle, he caught sight of a plume of smoke rising above the trees—from the direction of Willow's cabin.

His adrenaline pumping, he ran to the back of Toby's cabin and stashed his tools there, propping them against the side of the house. Then he charged toward the trail leading to Willow's property. He'd been on this trail before, but this time he plowed through it, leaping over gnarled roots and ignoring the branches that grabbed at his clothing and slapped his face.

Panting, he stumbled into the clearing that ringed her place. Lifting his head, he spotted a hooded figure running for the road. He started to give chase, the smell of the fire and some kind of chemical accelerant permeating his senses.

The dogs howling from the cabin stopped him short.

He let the assailant escape and spun around toward the flaming house. The smoke had intensified since he'd first noticed it, and his eyes stung as he battled his way to the front door. Fire engulfed the back of the cabin, and a window on the side of the house shattered, but the front door remained clear.

Heath snatched a log from beside the firepit and clutched it in both hands as he scrambled up the porch. He swung the log like a Louisville Slugger at the front window and smashed it in. The dogs could survive a few shards of glass. They wouldn't be able to survive this inferno.

He shoved his arm through the hole in the glass, and with his body halfway into the house, he reached around and unlocked the door. He pushed it in, and Luna rushed past him. Smoke billowed from the back of the house, and Heath called for Apollo.

The dog answered with a whine, and Heath followed the sound, almost tripping over him huddled in a corner of the room. Heath grabbed his collar. "It's okay, boy. Come out with me this way."

As he led Apollo to the front door, Heath heard sirens wailing and Luna's echoing cry. He got Apollo outside and corralled both dogs away from the house and the road where a fire truck careened to a stop. Helicopter blades thwacked above him as the chopper dumped red fire retardant into the trees at the edge of Willow's property. The sticky substance floated his way, and he threw an arm across his eyes.

As the firefighters rushed in, something exploded in the house, and another burst of flames shot from the roof. The chopper swooped in and doused the fire from above.

Heath tried to keep himself and the dogs away from the activity at the house. They had taken refuge beneath the picnic table, and he parked on top of it, pulling his shirt over his nose and mouth. They couldn't leave the area. He'd parked his truck on the other side, near the trail leading to Toby's house, and he couldn't take the dogs past the fire engines on the road. Right now, fear paralyzed them, but that same fear could send the dogs into a panic and out into the wilderness.

Heath lifted his head as footsteps approached him, and he raised his hand at Sheriff Chandler.

West stopped next to the table. "Are you okay? Do you need medical attention?"

"I'm fine." Heath held his arms in front of him. "Just a little sliced up from breaking the window. Nothing serious."

West asked, "Are you the one who called 911?"

"Never had a chance and don't think I can get service, anyway. I saw the smoke and ran over when I realized it was Willow's place. I saw someone running away from the fire, but I heard the dogs yelping and couldn't leave them."

West's brows shot up and disappeared beneath his hat. "You're kidding. You saw the arsonist?"

Spreading his arms, Heath asked, "You don't think this happened naturally, do you? Not after the break-in yesterday. Someone is trying to smoke Willow out—literally."

"Did you get a good look at this person?"

"Nope. He was running away. Had a black hoodie on, black pants. That's all I saw." Heath coughed. "If we can salvage the footage from Willow's security camera, you might get a look at him, but I doubt he was smiling for the camera."

"You sure the arsonist was male?"

"Are you thinking Ellie Keel is behind this?" Heath shrugged. "Could've been a woman."

A commotion erupted from the road, and Willow barreled into the clearing. "My dogs! My dogs!"

Hearing Willow's voice, Apollo lumbered from his spot beneath the table and trotted toward her.

Sobbing, she fell to her knees and wrapped her arms around her pet's neck. Willow wiped her nose on Apollo's fur and looked up. "Luna?"

"She's right here. Safe." Heath reached down and rubbed the top of Luna's head with his knuckles.

West cleared his throat. "Heath saw the arsonist running from the scene, Willow."

Her eyes widened. "Did you see who it was?"

"He was covered up. Disguised." Heath pushed to his feet. "Do you have any more questions for me, West? I think we need to get Willow away from here until the… rubble cools, and the dogs don't need to be here."

"Away from here?" Willow turned her head to take in the smoldering heap that used to be her summer home. "Where are we supposed to go?"

West snapped his fingers. "Why don't you stay with Astrid? She and her son have Sherlock. I'm sure she won't mind another couple of dogs, and I know Olly won't. Astrid's brother is still in DC, so she and Olly have the place to themselves."

"I'm not going to descend on Astrid."

Heath said, "Stay at my hotel. I know there are vacancies."

"The Bay View Hotel is not going to allow a couple of mangy mutts to roam their halls."

"If you don't want to stay at Astrid's, at least leave the dogs with her, and you go to the hotel." West adjusted his hat and glanced at the ruined cabin. "Might be a good idea for you to stay in town until things get…settled."

"I guess." Willow chewed her bottom lip. "You don't think Astrid would object?"

"Absolutely not." West pulled out his phone. "I'll call her now. You sure you don't need medical attention, Heath?"

"I'm good."

Willow turned her gaze on him for the first time since she rushed onto the scene. She studied him from his still-tearing eyes to his soot-stained shirt and his battered arms. "Why are you here, and how'd you save the dogs?"

"Saw the smoke, noted the direction and ran over. Heard the dogs yelping in the cabin, so I let the arsonist go to get the dogs." He pulled up the hem of his T-shirt to wipe his face. "You're welcome."

"I mean, yeah, thanks for rescuing the dogs. What

kind of person drugs dogs and then sets fire to a house with them in it?"

Heath eased out a long breath. "Someone desperate to chase you off this property. If you don't have a place to live here, maybe they think they can force you out."

"That's not gonna work with me." She dug her heels into the dirt and wedged her hands on her hips, looking like she'd never leave.

"Maybe they don't know who they're dealing with." He tugged on Luna's collar. "Let's get out of here. Breathing in all this stuff can't be healthy."

West strolled over from where he was talking to the fire captain. "Definitely arson. The perpetrator used accelerant. Captain Foster said you can come back tomorrow to sift through the remains. Much of the living room survived intact, although I'm sure the water got to some things. The firefighters pulled out and bagged your laptop."

Willow waved her hand. "All that stuff is on the cloud. At least the dogs are safe."

"Which reminds me. Astrid said she has no problem taking the dogs, and you're more than welcome to stay with them."

"As long as the dogs are secured, I'll stay at the Bay View."

"Let Astrid know if you change your mind." West held up a finger. "Let me get your laptop."

Willow urged Apollo toward the road. "I might just have to wait until all these vehicles leave before getting the dogs in my truck. Where's your truck? I didn't see any other vehicles on my drive."

"I left it up the road. I didn't know where the fire was headed or how fast."

Batting at a bit of floating ash, Willow asked, "Do you want me to take you to your truck on my way to dropping off the dogs?"

"No. You go ahead. I'll make sure there's a room waiting for you at the hotel. I think the fire captain wants to talk to me again anyway."

West walked toward them, a large plastic bag swinging from his hand. "The firefighters grabbed a few other things, too, some files on your table that looked important."

"Thank you." Willow took the bag from West and, with the sheriff and Heath's help, coaxed the dogs past the fire engines to her truck and into the bed, giving Apollo a boost.

Heath waved her off with a sense of relief. Then, with just a couple of firefighters left on the scene, he plunged back into the forest and retraced his steps to Toby's place. He'd have to come back later to continue digging. He stashed his tools in the back of his truck and drove to his hotel.

The ready smile on the hotel clerk's face vanished when Heath strode into the lobby. He must look worse than he felt.

"A-are you okay, Mr. Bradford?"

"You know that fire on the other side of the island? I was there."

The guy clicked his tongue. "I heard about it. Just glad it didn't start a forest fire."

"No, but it badly damaged my friend's cabin, and she's going to need a place to stay. Do you know Willow Sands?"

"I know of her. We'd be happy to offer her something here."

"Put her room on my credit card."

The clerk clicked his computer's keyboard and, without looking up from the screen, said, "We have a room on your floor, just a few doors down."

"Even better. You can give me the key card. I'm meeting her here in the lobby."

The clerk finished the transaction and slid two cards across the counter. "Let me know if we can do anything else for you or Ms. Sands."

Heath jerked his thumb toward the alcove stocked with drinks and snacks to the right of the front desk. "Put a couple of waters on my room, too."

After he gathered two bottles of water from the fridge in the little market, Heath dropped down on a sofa in the lobby, exhaustion rolling through his body. Confusion and frustration beat against his temples.

His father had sent him here to pressure Toby Keel and Willow Sands into selling their properties to Bradford and Son, so the company could work with the Samish to develop the land for a casino on the island. At the time, Heath's father had no idea that Heath would discover that Toby had been the one sending him anonymous messages about his mother. As soon as Heath figured that out, his mission on the island changed.

The mission also changed as soon as he met up again with Willow Sands.

His eyes flew open as someone touched him on the shoulder. "Sorry it took so long." Willow's voice was quiet. "Had to get the dogs settled, but I think they'll be okay there. They're getting all kinds of attention from Astrid's son."

"That's good." Heath sat up and rubbed his eyes. "Can't believe I just dozed off in a hotel lobby."

She sat beside him and squeezed his thigh. "You were a hero saving Apollo and Luna. I think you deserve some rest—and some first aid."

"Just a few cuts and scratches." He squinted at his arms. "And some singed hair. Don't know how that happened. I wasn't running through the flames."

"Well, I smell like an ashtray, and I wasn't there as long as you were. There was hot debris floating around. A few of those fire flakes probably landed on you." She called to the front desk. "Hello! Do you have a first aid kit? Just a few bandages, antiseptic and burn cream."

"We do. Take it up to your room and return it whenever. I'll go get it." The clerk disappeared in the back and then walked over to them with a white plastic first aid kit.

Heath said under his breath, "I think he wants me out of his lobby."

"Of course he does. You look a mess." She prodded his shoulder. "Your place or mine?"

"Mine. I can change my clothes, too." He handed her the key cards to her room, and they took the elevator up to the fourth floor, where her room sat a few doors down from his.

He flashed his card at the door and pushed it open. "You can check out your room. I'll be fine. Put your things away."

"No way." She squeezed past him and placed the first aid kit on the credenza, dropping the plastic bag West had given her. She flipped the kit open and rifled through the contents. "You should wash your injuries with soap and water first."

"Good idea." He walked into the bathroom and whistled. "No wonder I scared that hotel clerk. I look like hell."

"There's some burn ointment in here, some antibiotic cream, bandages, ibuprofen."

Heath pulled his T-shirt over his head and hitched it over the shower rod. He ran warm water in the sink and soaped up a washcloth with the bar. He ran it across the scratches and cuts on his hands and arms, wincing at the stings.

Blotting himself dry with a towel, he slung it over his shoulder, then splashed some water on his face. Finally, he ran his wet hands through his hair. The next best thing to taking a shower.

When he walked out of the bathroom, Willow was standing in front of an array of first aid items. She glanced up, and he felt the heat from her gaze that swept across his bare chest almost as intensely as he'd felt the fire in her cabin today.

Tapping the credenza, she said, "Burn ointment?"

"On the backs of my hands and a few spots on my neck."

"Sit." She nodded at the bed.

He perched on the edge of the mattress and held out his hands while she plucked up a white tube. She squeezed some gel on the tips of her fingers and dabbed at some red marks and blisters on his hands. Then she shuffled closer and tapped at a few spots on his throat.

She spun around suddenly and dropped the ointment on the credenza. "Do you need antibiotic cream for those cuts?"

He inspected the red welts on his arms and one slice where the glass from the window cut him. "Just on this one spot, I think. I can get that if you put a little cream on my hand."

"I got it." She turned back around, pinching another tube between her fingers. She leaned over him and patted some of the cream on the cut. "This one's different from the others. This one is a cut. The other smaller ones are scratches. You got those from reaching through the shattered glass?"

He got those from racing through the woods, and she probably suspected that. "No clue where those came from. They might even be old scratches."

Finished tending to his wounds, Willow packed up the first aid kit and ducked down to the mini fridge. She held up a beer. "I think you deserve this."

"Sure." Heath yawned. "Join me?"

"If you don't mind paying minibar prices for a bottle of beer."

"This could be considered a business meeting. I'll expense it." He gestured for the bottle, and she handed it to him.

While he stayed on the bed, she sat on the desk chair with her beer. "What do you think is going on? Why would someone set fire to my cabin?"

"Probably to put pressure on you." The few sips of alcohol trickled down to his nerve endings and dulled them. He'd been so tired the past few days, creeping out, digging holes. And he didn't even know what he was looking for. His lids felt heavy, but he took another slug of beer.

"Does this person or group think because I don't have a place to live on the island that I'll just give up?"

"How'd your meeting go with the attorney? Did he shed any light on the situation?"

"Not really. The property is legally mine according to the will, but it doesn't mean the Keels can't challenge." Willow picked at the label on her bottle, opened her mouth and then shut it. Whatever she was going to say, she'd decided against it.

He couldn't blame her for that. Plenty of secrets swirling around this island, and he didn't know if he could handle one more.

He finished off the beer in two more gulps and collapsed, flat on the bed, holding the bottle loosely in his hand. "I think that fire did me in. I was already tired, but that adrenaline spike drained me."

Willow took the bottle from his hand, and he heard her voice through a drowsy haze. "I'm going to let you get some sleep. You started the day tired, and it doesn't appear that it got any better for you. Thanks for booking the room."

As she closed the door with a whisper, he was already trailing off to sleep.

WILLOW THUMBED ON a light as she walked into her hotel room. She placed the plastic bag on the desk. It contained her laptop, Toby's files and a few toiletry items and food that Astrid had pressed upon her. She fished out her computer and a sandwich. She was actually more grateful that the firefighter saved those files than the laptop—especially after what she'd learned from her mother.

She plugged in the computer, and it flickered to life. She entered the Wi-Fi password from the hotel and launched a search engine. A quick probe confirmed that just because a person owned the surface of a property didn't mean that person also owned the mineral rights on that property.

Her exploration had also delivered the bad news that the

owner of the mineral rights could exploit those rights, regardless of the wishes of the property owner. Big trouble.

Who else knew about the nickel vein and that she
probably didn't own it?

She slumped in the chair and unwrapped the sandwich Astrid had packed for her. Peeking inside the pita
bread, Willow smiled. Knowing her preferences, Astrid
had slathered the pita with hummus and added some
diced tomato, onion and cucumber. What a mom.

She devoured the sandwich, then bit into an apple,
her leg bouncing up and down. After her cabin had been
ransacked and set on fire, she couldn't just sit here. Her
gaze wandered to the bottle of water Heath had procured
for her, and she grabbed it.

What had he been doing near her cabin? She'd taken
note of the road when she left for Astrid's and didn't
see his truck parked there. He must've been at Toby's
for some reason.

She noted the setting sun out the window, gulped back
some water and shoved the hotel key in her back pocket.
With both Lee and Heath nosing around that property,
she figured it was time she did her own reconnaissance
out there. She'd already signed the paperwork Jason had
given her. Hell, she owned that land.

Before she slipped out the door, she grabbed Toby's
files and shoved them into the hotel safe. She couldn't
trust anyone right now.

She made the forty-five-minute drive back across the
island and parked on the road that led to Toby's trail.
Tilting her head back, she sniffed as she hiked in, the
acrid odor of the fire still permeating the air.

By the time she reached the clearing where Toby's

cabin huddled, the sun had sent out its last rays, caught in the mist that hugged the ground. Willow's flashlight played over the front of the cabin. Had Heath broken into Toby's house after she and he had left earlier? Had he seen something during their search?

She stomped up the steps and tried the door. The knob resisted her attempts to turn it, and she didn't have her key. Hunching forward, she cupped her hand over the window and peered inside. Nothing looked disturbed or any different from this afternoon's visit. She turned around, and leaning against the door, she scanned the front of the property. The yellow caution tape had sunk to the ground, weighed down by the moisture in the air.

She descended the porch and circled behind the property. That was where Heath had come from on the night of Toby's death. Had he come back today to finish the business he started?

She flicked the light toward the two maples towering near the edge of the forest. Heath had seemed unusually interested in those trees today. In fact, his whole demeanor had changed after they left the cabin.

She was about to shine her light on the other side of the cabin when some lumpy objects on the ground near the trees caught her attention. Holding her flashlight in front of her, she crept toward the maples.

When her light picked up mounds of dirt next to several holes in the ground, she almost dropped her flashlight. Had Heath been digging out here? She didn't remember seeing this disruption a few nights ago. But had she walked back here? Maybe Toby had dug those holes.

She could think of only two reasons to dig holes in the ground: either you were burying something or retrieving something. She scuffed toward the pits and knocked some dirt back into one with the toe of her hiking boot as she peered down with her light. Dirt and more dirt.

Had the digger found what he was looking for? Or had a fire interrupted his search?

She knew where Toby kept his tools, and she crossed the back of the property to a dilapidated shed, its door hanging on one rusty hinge. She pulled open the door, which squealed in protest, and lit up the cobwebby interior with her light.

"Two can play this game." She grabbed a shovel, which had seen better days, leaning against the wall of the shed and dragged it outside. She tromped back to the site of the little treasure hunt, the shovel heavy on her shoulder.

She placed her flashlight on a log, pointing in the direction of the excavation area, and plunged the shovel in the dirt. As soon as the shovel met solid resistance, she knew why the initial excavator had stopped. You couldn't dig any farther once you hit the rock beneath the dirt.

She shuffled to the right and tensed her muscles to have another go. As she lifted the shovel, a loud popping noise startled her at the same time she felt something hot whiz by her ear.

Someone was shooting at her.

Chapter Ten

The sound of gunfire had Heath diving for cover on the trail, but Willow's scream juiced him up. He jumped to his feet and ran toward the sounds, pulling his own gun from his jacket pocket. When he reached the clearing of Toby's cursed property, he dropped to the ground again and army-crawled toward the cabin. He called out, "Willow! Are you okay, Willow?"

He got a muffled sob as an answer, and then… "I'm okay. Was that a gun?"

"That was a gun. Where are you?"

"I'm behind the house, over by the maple trees you noticed today."

Heath swore under his breath. "I'm by the cabin's porch. Can you crawl over here? Flat on the ground."

"Wh-what if the shooter comes out of the woods and finishes what he started?"

"I have a gun." He yelled loud enough for every creature in the forest to hear him. "Stay down. If someone comes out of those trees, I'll take care of him."

He heard scraping and scuffling noises, so he shimmied toward the back corner of the cabin. The rising moon shed enough light on the scene that he could see Willow make her way toward him.

When she reached his position, he wrapped an arm around her. "Sure you're okay?"

"No, I'm not okay, but I'm not hurt. Let's get the hell out of here."

He pushed her toward the trail that led to the road and duckwalked in a crouch behind her, his weapon ready for an assault. After a few feet of scrabbling along the forest floor, he poked her thigh. "Get up slowly and then run like hell. I've got your back."

Willow galloped through the woods like a sprightly fawn, leaping over roots and fallen logs, bobbing and weaving away from the branches that reached out for her. Heath followed her at a slower and much clumsier pace, but he kept his gun ready in case someone decided to come after them.

When Willow reached the road, she continued running to her truck, which he'd spotted earlier. When he'd seen it, he almost turned around, knowing full well she'd find the holes he'd dug previously. He was happy now he'd followed that sixth sense in his head, telling him to go after her.

When he caught up to her, bent over, hands on her knees, panting, he leaned against her truck. "What happened out there?"

She coughed. "I'm not talking here. Meet me in my hotel room. You have a lot of explaining to do."

He holstered his gun and tapped the phone in his pocket. "Should we call 911? Someone fired a weapon at you, and I doubt it was a stray hunter."

"Wild turkey hunting ended in the spring, and other game hunting doesn't start until fall. Summer is a no-go season, but I guess human prey is year-round." She grabbed his hand hovering over his pocket. "Don't call the police—at least, not until we talk."

"Fine by me." He blew out a long breath. The last thing he wanted to do was call the police and try to explain his excavation site on Toby Keel's property.

He followed her truck back to the hotel, with one eye on his rearview mirror checking for a tail. He didn't believe anyone would be following them—whoever shot at Willow knew exactly who she was and probably where she was staying. But did they know why she was digging? Had they been waiting for Heath to show up?

By the time he pulled into the hotel parking lot, next to Willow standing beside her truck, he'd decided to come clean to her. Why not? He didn't owe Toby Keel anything.

They walked side by side into the hotel, silently. When they got to the elevator, Heath turned to Willow. "Why'd you go out there tonight?"

The doors opened. Willow entered the car and jabbed the button for the fourth floor. "I didn't believe your story this afternoon. I figured you'd been at Toby's place again. I just didn't know why. I still don't know why."

When they got to her room, she sat on the edge of a chair, folding her arms.

He took the corner of the bed. "You know I was digging on Toby's land."

"What are you looking for?"

"My mother."

Willow's mouth dropped open, and she stopped kicking her leg. "Your mother is buried on Toby's property?"

"I don't know." The hand he plowed through his hair came away dusted with soot. He rubbed his palms to-

gether. "Toby knew something about my mother's disappearance. He started sending me cryptic notes several
months ago. When I pinned him down, shortly before I
showed up on Dead Falls Island, he told me that he and
my mother had been friendly. That they'd had a special
relationship."

"An intimate one?" Willow chewed on the side of her
thumb. "They were having an affair?"

"I'm not sure about that. He said my mother would
confide in him about her bad marriage, her unhappiness,
her depression. He tried to help her, but she was determined to kill herself."

"Wasn't much help. Do you believe him? Did he tell
you your mother committed suicide?"

He nodded as a sharp pain shot through the back of
his head. "He said she'd spent a lot of time at his place
to get away, and when he got home one day, he found
her dead."

Willow gasped and covered her mouth. "Why didn't
he call the police?"

"Because she told him she just wanted to disappear."
Hunching forward, he braced his elbows on his knees
and clasped his hands.

"And then what? He buried her behind his house. He
kept mum when everyone was looking for her." Willow
wound a strand of hair around her finger, her gaze never
leaving his face.

"He never claimed he buried her."

"Then why are you digging? Where is she?"

"That's what I was trying to find out the night he died.
I didn't go to his cabin to talk about the land deal. I told
him I wanted answers." He stood up and shoved his hand

in his pocket, withdrawing the frayed piece of paper. He thrust it toward Willow. "This was his last note to me."

She smoothed out the paper and read the words aloud. "'Where the mist meets the earth, between the giant maples.'"

"He told me I'd find my mother there. I don't know if he meant her actual body, something belonging to her, or if he just meant it metaphorically. I went to his cabin to find out."

"Oh my God, Heath." She crumpled the paper in her fist and moved from the chair to a position next to him on the bed. "That's terrible. He's evil for putting you through this, for playing games with you."

His heart thumped painfully in his chest. "Do you think he was playing games? Maybe this was all some sick joke to punish me for being Brad Bradford's son."

"Toby was a strange man. I don't think anyone ever really knew him. My father probably got the closest to him. Even my mother shared with me today that Toby was a womanizer. Got the impression he may have hit on her, too." She tossed the balled-up note onto the table. "Maybe your mom rejected his advances. Maybe this is his revenge on her, on you. Who knows?"

"I have to find out for myself." Heath pinched the bridge of his nose.

"And to do that, you're going to excavate Toby's property—I mean, my property."

"I didn't think it would be such a big deal to dig a few holes...but someone doesn't want me digging."

Clasping her hands between her knees, she twisted her head to look at him. "You mean that bullet wasn't meant for me?"

"I mean, someone has an eye on Toby's property, saw you digging and took a potshot at you. Maybe they didn't even mean to hit you. They just wanted to drive you away."

"Like the fire drove me away." She pulled her bottom lip between her teeth. "Do you think the two incidents are related? I'm the common denominator. It might not have anything to do with the holes. With Toby gone, why would anyone care about your mother? Sorry—except you, of course."

"I don't know." He pressed the heels of his hands into his eye sockets. He'd dozed off when Willow left his room but hadn't slept very long, his dreams compelling him to wake up and finish what he'd started.

Willow encircled his wrist with her fingers. "You know you still have soot in your hair and your hands. Now you're getting it all over your face, and you still look exhausted."

"This hasn't been the best day of my life." But her understanding and gentle touch had just made it a whole lot better.

"Have you even eaten since your heroic rescue of the dogs? Unless you grabbed something between your nap and your heroic rescue of me at the excavation site, I don't think so." She nudged him. "Go take a shower, and I'll order you some room service."

He pushed up to his feet. "428."

"What does that mean?" She jumped up and grabbed the phone by the side of the bed.

"That's my room number for the room service. Burger and fries are fine and another beer, unless you want to give me one from your minibar."

She placed two hands flat on his back and pushed

him. "You can clean up and eat here. That shooting incident still has me rattled. I'd rather not be alone right
now, and you do have a weapon."

"Are you sure?" He glanced at her bathroom door. He
didn't want to leave her alone, either, but his motivation
was purely selfish.

"I'm sure. I haven't even had time to use the shower
yet, so knock yourself out." She waved the phone at him.
"I'll order the food."

As she spoke into the phone, Heath toed off his shoes
and shut himself in the bathroom. He stripped off his
clothes and stepped under the warm spray of the shower,
the coils in his shoulders loosening for the first time today.

He should've told Willow sooner. It felt good to have
someone on his side.

WILLOW ORDERED THE food and collapsed into the chair.
Whatever motive she'd imagined Heath had for digging
those holes, looking for his dead mother was not on
her bingo card. What was Toby playing at? Had he told
Heath some tall tale about Jessica Bradford to distract
him from the land deal?

News like that would take Heath right out of the game
of pressuring Toby to sell his land—and it had. His meeting with Toby that night was supposed to be about his
mother, not the casino deal.

Was that another reason Toby didn't want to sell the
land? He didn't want the developers to make any dis-
coveries on his property, like a dead body.

With Toby dead, who else would want to stop that
discovery? Heath could be completely wrong about the
shooter. That bullet could've been meant for her, regard-

less of what she was doing. The fact that she was back on the land could've been motivation enough for someone to take a shot at her.

The shower stopped, and Willow held her breath. For a second, she'd thought Heath would refuse her offer of showering and eating in her room. He had a perfectly good shower two doors down. She knew playing to his protective instincts would get him to stay.

Was she really afraid to stay here by herself? She didn't believe the shooter or the arsonist, whether that was the same person or not, would track her down to the hotel and finish his business, but it eased her mind to have Heath here.

The hair dryer whirred from behind the closed door, and Willow shut her eyes for a second, indulging in the fantasy of Heath Bradford naked in her bathroom. That vision could keep her warm on a cold, rainy Seattle night.

The door cracked open, and Heath stuck his head into the room. "Is the food here yet?"

She spied a lot of bare skin in the sliver of that opening and swallowed. "Not yet. Take your time."

Five minutes later, when he stepped out of the bathroom on a cloud of citrus-scented steam, he'd left just his feet bare. The T-shirt and clean pair of jeans he'd changed into after the fire covered the rest of him.

He cocked his head back and forth as if releasing a kink in his neck. "That feels better. I'm halfway to human."

"Eating a cow is going to complete the process?"

"I think that should about do it."

"Start with one of these." She held out a cold beer to him, the cap popped.

Studying the label on the bottle, he said, "I don't know. The last time I drank one of these, it knocked me out, and you sneaked back to Toby's to find out what I was up to."

"You were dead on your feet then. You've been revived by a gunshot." She clinked the neck of her bottle against his and took a gulp of beer.

The knock on the door startled them, and they both rose to answer. Heath held out a hand. "I'll get it."

Pressing a hand against the door, he peered through the peephole first and then stepped back to open it.

A hotel employee rolled a cart, a white tablecloth flapping around it, into the room and parked it by the window. After he transferred the contents of the cart to the table, Heath thanked him and handed him a wad of cash.

When Heath saw the waiter out of the room, he returned and whipped the silver domes off the two plates. He snatched a french fry from a heap of them stacked next to a mile-high burger and nudged the other plate, overflowing with a garden salad, in her direction. "Is this yours?"

"It actually came with the burger and fries. It's all yours." She wrinkled her nose.

"Did you eat before swinging your shovel at the ground?" He rubbed his hands together and pulled a chair up to the table, setting his beer next to the plate of food on the tray.

"Astrid packed some food for me when I dropped off the dogs."

"Nuts and berries?" He cut into the burger, and pink juices flooded the plate.

"Hilarious." She jabbed a finger at the mess on his plate. "I ordered you a medium rare. Too pink?"

"It's perfect." He tapped the edge of the salad plate with his fork. "Help yourself. I doubt I'm going to eat that."

Picking up a fork, she took the seat to his left. "Do you need this fork?"

"I'm a real man. I eat with my hands." He pounded his chest.

"Okay, Tarzan."

She let him eat in peace as she picked at the salad. This was the most relaxed she'd seen him all day. Why would Toby tell him he could find his mother here on the island? It seemed almost like torture.

Heath practically inhaled one half of the burger and started on the second half. He washed a bite down with his beer and said, "Do you want some fries?"

"I'm fine." She dabbed her mouth with a napkin. "Are you going to keep digging? What if you don't find anything?"

"I'll keep digging. My father was satisfied to have my mother declared dead a few years ago, but I can't let go as easily as he did."

"What exactly does he think happened to your mother?"

"He believes she committed suicide and made sure nobody found her body." He pushed away his plate with the rest of his burger.

She'd meant to allow him to eat without dwelling on his mother or Toby's sadistic clues. She picked up one of the fries and nibbled on the end. "Why would she do that?"

"I don't know." He raised and dropped his shoulders quickly. "My father said she always threatened to go out that way. And I'm not saying my father was lying. My mother was an unstable woman, but you know..."

"I do know. She's still your mom." She plucked up another fry and held it out to him. "I'm sorry. I didn't mean to ruin your appetite. Finish your food."

His gaze shifted from the french fry in her hand to her eyes as he leaned forward and opened his mouth. She put the fry to his lips, and he took in the whole thing, his salty lips meeting the tips of her fingers.

She didn't snatch her hand away. Instead, she traced his mouth with the pad of her finger.

His whiskey eyes darkened. "Would you kiss me now, even though I just ate a hamburger?"

She raised her eyes to the ceiling. "I think my vegetarian taste buds could handle that."

Tossing his napkin onto the tray, he stood up and circled behind her chair. He leaned over her, tilted her head back and kissed her upside down. He deepened the kiss, stroking her neck with his hand as her heart thundered in her chest.

She'd imagined a few kisses from Heath Bradford—then and now—but even her fantasies never felt like this. A tingling sensation started in her toes and buzzed through her entire body, although his mouth never left hers and his hand didn't trail down any farther than her throat.

Straightening up, he moved his hands to her shoulders, tucked them beneath her sweater and massaged her skin. The touch of his hands against her flesh set the blood in her veins afire, and the heat coursed through her body.

Closing her eyes, she released a sound from the back of her throat—something between a sigh and a groan.

He returned to the front of her chair and knelt before her. "You don't know how long I've wanted to touch you."

She touched the dark stubble on his jaw. "Two days?"

Running his hands along the outsides of her thighs, he said, "A lot longer than that. I was just a stupid kid who didn't know how to approach the most fascinating girl I'd ever encountered."

Her lips twisted into a smile. "I'm sure your popular friends would've had a lot to say if you'd started dating the Tree Girl."

"Maybe. I wasn't as bold or independent as you. Following the clues to my mother's disappearance instead of doing my father's bidding is the closest I've come to rebelling against him."

"Is that what this is?" She cupped his jaw. "Seducing me to get back at Daddy?"

"This is—" he kissed her forehead "—me—" he kissed her cheek "—seducing you—" he kissed her throat, where her pulse throbbed "—because I want you more than anything right now."

She draped her arms over his shoulders. "Then be bold and independent and take me."

With a grin on his face and a light in his eyes, Heath scooped her off the chair and hoisted her in his arms. She wrapped her legs around his waist as he carried her to the bed. He swung around so that he was sitting on the edge of the mattress with her curled around his body.

He sealed his mouth over hers in a kiss that seared her soul, his pent-up longing drowning her previous reservations about him, about her feelings for him, her long-smoldering desire for the teenage boy leaping to an urgent need for the adult man.

Heath brushed a loose strand of hair away from Willow's face, his touch gentle and full of affection. His thumb traced a delicate path along her cheek, and she closed her eyes, savoring the sensation.

Willow placed her hands against Heath's chest, feeling the steady rhythm of his heart beneath her fingertips, his body heat ferocious beneath the material of his shirt. She pulled the shirt over his head and tossed it over her shoulder.

She dipped her head and placed a trail of kisses along his collarbone, skimming her teeth along his flesh.

He fell against the bed, and she straddled him as he unbuttoned her shirt and peeled it from her shoulders. She unhooked her bra for him, and his hands cupped her breasts. He ran the pads of his thumbs over her peaked nipples, and she squirmed against him.

He sucked in a breath. "You're driving me crazy."

Curling his hands around her waist, he lifted her from his lap and positioned her on the bed next to him. His clumsy fingers grappled with the button on her jeans, and she swatted away his hands.

"We'll be here all night if I leave this to you."

"What's wrong with that?" With a much defter touch, he unbuttoned his own jeans and pulled them off, along with his black briefs.

She left her jeans gaping as she drank in the sight of his naked body stretched out on the bed. "I'm pretty sure you didn't look like this in high school."

"I didn't." He tugged on a lock of her hair hanging over her shoulder. "Now who's taking too long?"

She whipped off her jeans and snuggled next to him. Heath's hands moved to the small of her back, drawing her closer until there was no space left between them. Their bodies molded together, fitting perfectly like pieces of a long-lost puzzle. Their lips met again with a newfound urgency, a shared yearning fueled by the danger and uncertainty of the past few days and the desire to connect with someone safe.

As their kisses deepened, the room seemed to disappear for Willow, leaving only the two of them, lost in each other's embrace. Dead Falls Island, the land, Toby, the secrets, all of it faded into insignificance, and all that mattered was the two of them in this moment.

Heath's hands roamed across her body, and he brought her to climax with his touch. Before the haze of content completely settled, she reached for him and guided him inside, where he opened her and filled her at the same time, bringing her a sense of completeness.

As he plunged into her over and over, she curled her fingers into his backside, digging her nails into his flexing muscle. He released, and she wrapped her legs around him, riding him until the end. They lay side by side, their limbs entwined, murmuring silly things to each other until they drifted off.

What seemed like seconds later, Willow jerked awake. She squinted at the clock to discover they'd been asleep for about an hour.

Heath's arm draped heavily over her hip, and Willow scooted away, trying not to wake him. His nighttime excursions had left him exhausted. She didn't want to keep the poor guy awake, even though her greedy gaze skimmed across his body splayed on the bed.

She tiptoed to the bathroom to freshen up. Then she yanked one of the fluffy white hotel robes from a hook on the door and wrapped herself in it before returning to the main room.

She cleaned up Heath's meal from the table and set the tray on the floor outside the door in the hallway. She grabbed a water from the mini fridge and sat down at the table, sliding Toby's file folders in front of her.

The game Toby and Heath were playing explained why Heath had been interested in entering Toby's cabin with her, but she got to his files first. If Toby did have anything about Jessica Bradford in his papers, she'd share it with Heath. She couldn't imagine what he'd been going through. At least when her mother took off, Willow had known exactly why and where she'd been headed.

The desk lamp illuminated the top of the folder she'd thumbed through before. It contained receipts and not much more. By the time she reached the third file, things got more interesting. It held legal documents about the property, verifying the terms of Toby's possession.

With a renewed sense of determination and Heath breathing heavily behind her, she dived into the next folder. Her pulse picked up when she recognized documents containing geologist reports and maps. Toby knew about the nickel on the property. Had her father left the rights to Toby but not the property? If so, Toby's attorney, Jason Hart, didn't know anything about it.

When she got to the bottom of the sheaf of papers, Willow's heart skipped a beat. She picked up a document and held it beneath the lamp. It was a mineral deed.

She scanned the legalese until she reached a name at the bottom. An icy finger seemed to stab her chest when she read the name, and her gaze slowly turned to the man sleeping in her bed—the man who owned the mineral rights to her property.

Chapter Eleven

A bright light flashed down on him, and Heath squeezed his eyes, seeing black dots behind his lids. An insistent voice prodded his eardrums in time to a determined prodding of his shoulder.

"Wake up. You knew. You knew all this time."

Willow's words pierced his sleep haze, and he peeled one eye open to find her hovering over him like an avenging angel, her lips pursed and a glint in her eye. He'd remembered a much different look on her face when he made love to her.

He closed his eye again and rubbed it. When he opened both, the same sight still met his gaze. He pulled the tangled sheet over the bottom half of his body. "What? What's going on?"

"This." Clutching a piece of paper in her fist, she waved it in his face. "The mineral deed to my property. *My* property."

"Okay." His eyes darted around the room looking for the punch line. "The mineral deed?"

"You knew. All this time you knew, and that's why you were digging around." She crumpled up the paper and threw it at him. "You didn't have to dig. It's on the map. It's all on the map."

Heath sat up, scrunching up a pillow behind his back. "I don't know what you're talking about, Willow. You're going to have to start at the beginning."

"Me? Why don't you start at the beginning—the beginning where you bamboozled my father out of those rights."

"I didn't bamboozle your father out of anything. Can we just…? Can I just…?" He plucked at the sheet covering his nakedness. "Let me put some clothes on."

"Please do." She crossed her arms and pivoted toward the window as he staggered from the bed.

He swept up his jeans and briefs on his way to the bathroom. He splashed some water on his face, sluiced back his hair and rinsed out his mouth for good measure.

When he eased open the door, he felt as if he was entering the lion's den. What had set her off? What mineral rights was she talking about?

"Is it safe?" He poked his head into the room.

Willow spun around, dragging her hair into a ponytail and clutching it like she was about to pull it out. "I dug through Toby's paperwork some more and found something very interesting."

"Obviously. Something about mineral rights on Toby's land."

"I already knew about that." She waved her hand up and down in his direction. "You can put your shirt on, too."

"Okay." This must be bad. He stepped over the bedcovers in disarray on the floor, his head down in search of his T-shirt.

"Here it is." She ducked down and picked up his shirt

where she'd thrown it before in a moment of passion. She chucked it at him, and he caught it in one hand.

A different kind of passion had her enflamed now.

He pulled the shirt over his head. "You already knew about mineral rights on the land? You didn't tell me that."

"I didn't—" She scooped up the crumpled piece of paper from the floor and bobbled it in her hand. "I didn't want to tell anyone just yet. Didn't want the property to become even more valuable to outsiders, but now I know."

"What is it you think you know?"

"You own the mineral rights, and you were aware of that all along." The finger she leveled at him felt like a poke in his eyeball.

"Honestly, Willow. I have no idea what you're talking about. I didn't know Toby's property had any minerals on it and neither did Bradford and Son." The last words stuck in his throat. Had his father known? "What kind of minerals are we talking about?"

She spit out one word. "Nickel."

"Can I see the paper?" He held out his hand, and she slammed the balled-up wad into his palm.

He picked open the mass and smoothed it on the table. "A mineral deed. I've seen a few of these with some other land deals—not this one, though."

"Keep reading, all the way to the bottom."

He ran his finger over the legal verbiage until he reached his own name at the bottom of the page. "I'll be damned."

"That's all you have to say about it?" She narrowed her eyes, and her nostrils flared. "Why were you digging? All you had to do was visit some county clerk's office to get the maps and a copy of this deed. Toby has the map, too. I'm sure it details the location of the ore deposits."

"I'm sure I could have, and I'm sure the map is useful—except I didn't know that I had the mineral rights. Look—" he drilled a finger into the middle of the paper "—if I'd known about this, I would've already played that card to get the property over to Bradford and Son. Can you imagine the leverage I'd have?"

"Do have." Her chin jutted forward. "The leverage you *do* have, Heath."

"I don't care about that now. I want you to believe me, Willow. I knew nothing about any nickel on that property. I was digging because Toby was sending me mysterious notes about my mother's disappearance. If you don't believe me, you can go out and have a look at the Misty Hollow property. I was digging there first before you told me Toby referred to his property as *where the mist meets the earth*. I thought that clue meant Misty Hollow."

She sank onto the edge of the tousled bed like a deflated balloon. Maybe he'd gotten through to her. Covering her face, she fell back. "Make it make sense. Why would my father deed his property over to Toby with the stipulation that upon his death the surface property go to me, while knowing all the while that he'd already deeded the mineral rights to the same property over to you?"

"Wait." He picked up the paper and brought it close to his face. "Your father or Toby left the mineral rights to me?"

"It must've been my father. I don't think he gave Toby that kind of control over the property. Toby didn't have the power to leave the property to whomever he wanted, and I'm sure the mineral rights were already tied up."

"Why would he do that?" Heath hunched over the open folder and paged through the rest of the papers. Willow had been correct. Several of these pages contained maps. Who else knew about this?

"You tell me." She rolled onto her side, propping her head up, chin in hand. "You were the one having secret conversations with him when you were a teen."

"Secret conversations? H-he was just helping me out at the time I lost my mother." Heath's nose stung, and he cleared his throat. He was done showing vulnerability to Willow. "Your father was an adult voice of reason and compassion, someone who wasn't my father. We certainly never discussed property. I probably even told him I had no intention of going into business with my father and Bradford Associates."

"Yeah, how'd that go? Bradford Associates is now Bradford and Son. Bet my father never imagined that."

He cut a hand through the air. "Let's just stop with the accusations for a second. We don't even know if these documents Toby had are legal. You saw his cabin. Complete mess. This stuff could be old and out-of-date."

"There's a way we can find out. I've been doing a little research on mineral rights since I discovered the land contained these nickel deposits."

"When Toby's lawyer told you about the mineral rights, why couldn't he tell you who owned them then? Why the big secret?"

She swung her legs off the bed and planted her feet on the floor. "Jason Hart's not the one who told me."

"Then someone else does know about this. Who told you?"

"My mother."

His head snapped to attention. "Why didn't she tell you I owned the rights?"

She lifted her shoulders to her ears. "She didn't know you did. She just assumed I was in the know and would inherit the rights along with the property, but she didn't seem surprised that I didn't have a clue about the nickel."

"Your father, Toby, my father—why all the secrets?" He scuffed his knuckles against his chin.

Did his father know about the mineral rights? He found it hard to believe Brad Bradford wouldn't research every aspect of every property that came across his desk for a deal. And knowing about the rights, he must know who owned them. That kind of information was public record, but you had to know about it to look for it. His father had his ways.

Willow hopped up from the bed and took a turn around the room, tightening the belt on the robe that enveloped her small frame. "Do you think Toby was leading you on a wild-goose chase in a search for your mother when all along he knew about the nickel? Maybe he wanted you to dig to find the nickel deposits."

Heath's gut churned. "That's assuming I'd know what a nickel deposit looked like if I plunged my shovel into it. I wouldn't have any idea. I was a business major, not a geology major. I don't know how Toby could expect me to dig a hole on his property and say *eureka*! And why would he even go that route? If he wanted me to know I owned the mineral rights on his property, he should've told me."

"How does this affect the casino deal?" Willow reached past him to grab a bottle of water next to the files on the desk. How long had she been awake, poring over these documents?

"I would think this would put an end to the casino deal. I mean, if whoever owns the mineral rights, and I'm not saying it's me, decides to exploit the nickel, that would end any plans for hotels and restaurants to support the casino." Heath smacked the table with his palm. "I think that's the first order of business. We need to find out who really owns those mineral rights."

"And if it is you?" Willow's gaze never left his face as she tipped the bottle into her mouth.

"Before anything else, I wanna know why. Why would your father put those rights in my name?" He drummed his thumbs against the edge of the desk. "Something happened on this island at the time my mother disappeared, maybe even before, and it's now rearing its ugly head, causing mayhem and violence. We need to sort it out before someone else gets hurt."

"Maybe it's the sorting out that'll get someone hurt."

"It could be, but we have to take that risk." He rose from the table, pushing the folders away from him. He grabbed his shoes and headed for the door.

Willow called after him, "Y-you're going back to your own room?"

He kept plodding toward the exit, his gaze straight ahead, willing himself not to turn around. "We both need to get some sleep. We'll attack this tomorrow."

"Heath, what about…what about what happened between us?"

He pressed down on the handle of the door and yanked it open. "I think that was a mistake."

THE FOLLOWING MORNING, Willow stood in front of the mirror brushing her teeth. She'd screwed up big-time last night. She'd seen that deed with Heath's name and lost it. If only she'd taken a breather before shining a spotlight in his face to wake him up like the grand inquisitor.

What he'd said made sense. If he was already aware that he held the mineral rights to the property, he wouldn't be digging little holes in the ground. He would use the map and do a proper survey.

Of course, he could've known about the nickel deposits *and* be searching for his mother. She spit in the sink and rinsed her mouth. Even after making love with him last night, she still had her doubts. What he'd said on his way out the door was right. Having sex with Heath had been a big mistake.

From here on out, they'd better keep their relationship in the business zone. At least he still felt comfortable including her in his search for answers. His answers could turn out to be her answers. Someone had searched her place, burned it down and taken a shot at her. That couldn't be because Heath owned the mineral rights to her property, but she felt the two were somehow connected.

Her cell phone rang in the main room, and she jumped. When Heath left last night, he promised they'd attack this together but hadn't mentioned who would call whom. Her heart dropped when she spun the phone around to face her and saw her insurance company calling her back.

While she finished relaying the details of the fire to her insurance agent, someone tapped on her door. She wrapped up the call and peeked through the hole. She eased out a long breath when she saw Heath on the other side.

She flung open the door. "It's safe."

He gave her a tight smile and held up a white bag and a cardboard tray containing two cups. "Bagels and coffee—chai tea for you, if you drink it."

"I do, thanks." She ushered him into the room, relieved she'd taken the time to straighten the bedcovers after their roll in the hay last night. They didn't need that awkwardness between them right now.

He set the bag on the table and took one of the cups. "I did a little research last night when I got back to my room."

So while she'd been tossing and turning, alternately reliving and anguishing over their moments together, he'd been...researching. "I'll bet you did," she murmured under her breath.

Raising his eyebrows, he said, "Sorry?"

She coughed. "That's good. What did you discover?"

"I found out that we can research mineral rights on the Mineral and Land Records System website. You can also get the same information faster if you go to the county records office."

"Faster? Our county records office is on San Juan, isn't it?" She popped the lid from her tea and inhaled its spicy aroma before taking a sip.

"Literally a fifteen-minute flight from Dead Falls Island."

"I know you haven't lived here for a while, but San Juan Airlines doesn't make that trip every hour, or even every day."

"I've already arranged the flight." He snapped his fingers. "Private pilot is taking us over in about an hour. Will you be ready?"

She glanced down at her jeans, still smudged with soot from yesterday. "I was hoping to buy a few clothes this morning in case mine are burned to a crisp or water-logged."

"We can stop somewhere on the way to the airport." He opened the white bag and shook out a little container of cream cheese and some packets of butter. "That's why I brought breakfast with me, so we could get going."

"Are they expecting us at the county office?" She flat-tened a paper napkin on the table and hooked her finger around a poppy seed bagel from the bag.

"I arranged that, too." He claimed the remaining bagel and dug a plastic knife into the cream cheese. "I just need to bring my ID and a legal description of the prop-erty, which you should have from Jason Hart, right?"

"I'll bring my whole set of documents from Jason if that's what it takes." She smeared some cream cheese on one half of her bagel and scraped off some poppy seeds with her fingernail. "I'm sorry about last night—not the first part. I'm sorry about the second part…later. When I saw your name on that mineral deed, I don't know. I kinda saw red."

"You jumped to the worst conclusion…about some-one you just slept with." He took a big bite of his bagel, and the cream cheese squished out the sides. He had to lick it off with his tongue—damn him.

She closed her eyes to block out the sight of his tongue and the sensations it stirred up in her belly…and below. "I think that's why I went there."

"You normally interrogate men in your bed?" His tongue darted from his mouth, catching a crumb in the corner of it.

He was just torturing her now, and she deserved it.

"No. I guess my first thought was that you'd taken advantage of me, that you'd kept this secret from me."

He dropped his bagel. "You think I took advantage of you last night?"

"Not at all." She'd meant to apologize, and she'd made the situation worse. Her awkwardness with boys... men...had never left her. "I have an issue with feeling that love and affection are always given in exchange for something else. It's my go-to in relationships, which explains my single status."

The lines bracketing his mouth softened. "I get it. Are you going to eat that bagel or dismantle it?"

"Eat it."

They finished their breakfasts, and Willow grabbed her purse, shoving the documents inside. They took Heath's truck to the airport and stopped on the way at a vintage clothing store.

As they walked up to the entrance of Second Hand Sadie, Heath eyed the beaded cocktail dress in the window. "Are you sure about this?"

"I've shopped here before, and I know they have some jeans and tops I can scoop up." She waved to Sadie at the counter. "Hi, Sadie. I need an outfit that I can wear out of the store."

Sadie came around the counter and gave Willow a hug scented with patchouli. "I heard about your cabin. First Toby and now you. What's going on out there?"

"Have you heard anything more about Toby's death?"

Willow glanced at Heath. Had West been holding out on them?

"Just through the grapevine. You know everyone around here likes drama. Apparently, someone from that greedy development corps, Bradford and Sons, is out here, nosing around for land, and he murdered Toby to get his hands on it."

Willow covered her smile as Heath raised a hand. "That would be me."

"Sadie, this is Heath Bradford, and he's not all that greedy."

Sadie turned pink up to the roots of her pink hair. "Foot in mouth. I'm sorry, but you know how locals are."

"I know, and it's okay. We *are* nosing around for land—but we don't murder people."

Willow laughed. "Okay, let's forget about this greedy bastard for a few minutes and find me some clothes to wear."

Fifteen minutes later, dressed in a pair of bell-bottom jeans and a blouse with geometric shapes on it, Willow emerged from the dressing room. "I'll take this and throw in the denim trucker jacket in case this glorious sun goes away."

"It's Dead Falls Island—guaranteed to go away at some point today." Sadie patted a stack of clothes on the counter. "These, too?"

"Might as well. I'm not sure when I'm going to go back to my place and what my wardrobe's going to look like."

"And to prove I'm not a greedy bastard, I'll pay for Willow's stuff." Heath reached for his wallet and pulled out several bills.

"You don't have to do that. Sadie doesn't think you're greedy. Do you, Sadie?"

"No, but if a hot guy wants to buy you some clothes, girl, you let him." Sadie snatched the money from Heath's fingers and gave him change.

As they walked back to his truck, a plastic bag from the store swinging from his fingertips, Heath said, "Wow, this is a tough crowd. How do they feel about the Samish developing their land?"

"Most aren't happy about it, some are, and some believe the Samish can do whatever they want with their land, including building a casino. There are some Samish who disagree, too. Toby was obviously one of them. So no matter what Lee says, he doesn't speak for the entire Samish nation on this island."

They settled in the truck, and Heath punched on the ignition. "I wish the medical examiner would announce a manner of death for Toby. If the DFSD announces Toby's death was an accident, it will quell some of the suspicion."

"Including ours, but someone still searched my place and set fire to it. Those incidents have to be related to Toby's death, accident or not."

"His death could've definitely precipitated those actions. Maybe someone already knew Toby's land was going to you, and when he died, you became the focus of the intimidation."

"Lucky me."

They drove past the harbor to the small airport on the island. Several private planes, and some for hire, sat on the tarmac, ready to puddle jump to other islands and even to Seattle.

As Heath parked his truck, he pointed to a Cessna with red stripes. "That's ours."

"Fifteen minutes, huh?" Willow eyed the small plane and the man under the wing.

"Up and down. No time for complimentary drink service."

Five minutes later, they approached the plane. The person who'd been tinkering with it turned and wiped his hands on his overalls. "Heath Bradford?"

"Yeah. Thanks for taking us on short notice." Heath shook hands with the pilot. "Willow, this is Captain Mark Santos. He's flying us to San Juan today."

"Captain." Willow gingerly took his still-oily hand.

"Sorry about that." Mark glanced at his palms. "There are some wipes in the plane, and you can call me Mark. I'm just finishing my preflight. You can go on board."

They climbed onto the plane and took two of the four available seats. Must've cost Heath a bunch of cash to charter this plane to San Juan, but if the nickel in the rocks beneath that property really was worth millions, and he owned the rights, he could afford it.

As they settled into their seats and secured their seat belts, Heath handed her a headset. "Can get noisy in these things."

Nodding, Willow took the headset with a smile that masked her anxiety, but the plane took off smoothly, with just a few bumps and dips. Willow eased back in her seat as the emerald jewel of Dead Falls Island receded and other islets dotting Discovery Bay emerged through the mist.

The landing proved to be a tad rougher, and she didn't

uncurl her fingers from the armrest until the pilot rolled to a stop.

Heath squeezed her hand. "Not so bad, huh?"

She licked her lips and unhitched the seat belt. "How far to the county seat?"

"Far enough to take an app car."

They clambered out of the plane, thanking Mark, and Heath pulled out his phone to find them a ride. Fifteen minutes later, they were on the way to the county courthouse.

Heath approached the counter with authority, or at least as someone who had an appointment. When a clerk at another window called him, Heath tugged on Willow's sleeve. "Come with me."

The woman behind the glass smiled, her eyes crinkling at the edges. "After your call, Mr. Bradford, I was able to look up the records."

He said, "Great. Is the information clear-cut, or so bogged down in legalese, I'm gonna need my business degree to decipher it?"

"I don't think you'll have any problem figuring out that you're the legal owner of the mineral rights on that property, currently owned by Toby Keel."

"Not anymore." Willow clenched her teeth. It was all true. Her father had deeded the mineral rights on her property to Heath, a kid he'd talked to a few times.

"Sorry?" The woman tilted her head like a bird and shoved her glasses up the bridge of her nose.

"Toby Keel passed away. I'm the owner of the surface property." The corner of Willow's eye twitched.

"Well, that's perfect, then." The chirpy clerk grinned from ear to ear. "A husband-and-wife team."

Heath had the nerve to chuckle, and Willow felt like elbowing him in the ribs. Easy for him to find humor in the situation. He'd just discovered he owned mineral rights worth a fortune.

"I made you a copy of the documents." The clerk patted a manila envelope before sliding it beneath the window. "Did you lose the other set?"

"Other set?" Heath paused, the envelope clutched to his chest. "What do you mean? This is the first set I've ordered."

"Hmm, well." The clerk adjusted her glasses and peered at the computer monitor next to her. "That's not what I show here."

"Your records show that Heath Bradford ordered this report before?"

"Not exactly. Not *Heath* Bradford but Bradford and Son. Yes, it's right here. Bradford and Son already got a copy of the deed."

Chapter Twelve

Heath felt like Muhammad Ali just landed a punch to his gut, and it took all his control not to stagger back. He opened his mouth, but he couldn't form a sentence or utter a word.

Willow cleared her throat. "The corporation Bradford and Son requested these documents? When?"

The clerk's gaze shifted back to her computer screen. "About six months ago. It was done online, though. Is there a problem? Mineral rights are part of the public record. Anyone with the correct data can look up deeds for any property."

"Yeah, I know that. No problem." Heath held up the manila envelope in a surprisingly steady hand and said, "Thanks for your help."

Willow took his arm as they left the building but kept mum. He appreciated her silence. She could've laid into him with an *I told you so*.

When they reached the sidewalk, Heath took a couple of breaths of salty air. "What the hell just happened in there?"

"You're the proud owner of a vein of nickel, worth millions, running beneath my property, and there's not

a damned thing I can do to stop you from mining it."
She steered him down the sidewalk. "We might as well
have some lunch while we're here."

"Don't play dumb. That part didn't surprise me. After
looking at Toby's files, I figured they were legit. But how
and why was Bradford and Son looking at this stuff six
months ago, and why didn't my father tell me?"

He'd stopped in the middle of the sidewalk, and she
pulled him forward.

"Lunch and maybe an adult beverage before I get
back on that little death trap again." She pulled out her
phone. "My turn. There are a bunch of restaurants near
Friday Harbor."

Like a sleepwalker, he got into the rideshare and sat
in the back seat, his arms folded around the envelope.
"Six months. Little Miss Sunshine back there said the
docs were ordered six months ago, right?"

"That's what I heard. What's the significance of that?"

"Six months ago is when Toby started sending me
those cryptic notes, only I didn't know it was him back
then."

"How *did* you figure that out? Did he confess?"

Squeezing the back of his neck, Heath said, "I know
it sounds crazy, but I recognized his writing."

"You're right. It sounds crazy." Willow rapped on
the window. "Yeah, this is good. We'll find something
from here."

The driver dropped them off at the top of a long street
that led to the harbor, lined with tourist shops, bars and
restaurants. After perusing a few menu boards outside,
they agreed on a place that smelled like fresh fish, with
a sunny patio facing the water and the boats.

Once seated with menus and water in front of them, Willow picked up the conversation where they'd left off. "How'd you know it was Toby?"

"My father handed me the files on the two properties—yours and Toby's—and asked me to start preparing offers. Toby's file contained a lot of handwritten notes, most of them telling Bradford to go to hell. When I looked at that writing, which is distinctive, and pulled out the anonymous notes I'd been receiving, they were a match."

"That's crazy, Heath." Willow glanced up at the waitress. "I'll have a mimosa, please, heavy on the champagne, and a caprese salad."

Heath ordered a bottle of beer and a plate of fish-and-chips. Then he slumped in his seat and downed half the water. "Now I'm wondering if my father knew about those notes."

"You never told him?"

"Nope." He ran a hand through his hair. "Did he want me to go digging around for my mother with false hope? What kind of sick SOB puts his son through that?"

"Why wouldn't your father tell you about the mineral rights? Seems to me that would be a done deal for getting his hands on that property."

"Maybe because he thinks I wouldn't go along with exploiting those rights. Maybe because developing the property is more lucrative than decimating it to get to some nickel." He nodded to the waitress as she set their drinks on the table. "I'm going to find out. My father is conveniently on vacation right now, but I can reach him."

Willow held up her champagne flute. "I don't even know what to toast right now."

"How about our joint ownership of Toby's property?"

He clinked his bottle with her glass. "Nobody does anything to that property without our say-so."

"Without *your* say-so." Willow took a sip of her mimosa and crinkled her nose against the bubbles hopping from the glass. "From what I understand about mineral rights, you can choose to exploit those rights, regardless of the property owner's wishes."

"That's true, but I don't want to do anything against the property owner's wishes." He ran a thumb across her knuckles, reveling in the touch of her skin. His pride had forced him to storm out of her hotel room last night, but other parts of his psyche…and his body…wanted to stay with her all night long.

"What about your father's wishes? The wishes of Bradford without the Son?" She circled her finger in the air.

"Without the Son, Bradford's wishes don't count, especially after the underhanded way he went about the entire deal. Why wouldn't he tell me I owned those mineral rights?"

He didn't want to admit to Willow that his father kept him out of the loop on many aspects of their business. His father had brought him in as his partner, but he never treated him like one.

"Do you want my take?" Willow paused to thank the waitress as she delivered the colorful salad and delicious-smelling fish-and-chips.

"Of course…" Heath whipped his napkin into his lap. "…partner."

"Your father probably wants to buy time to wear you down, to work on you. If you believe he wants to develop the land more than he wants to exploit the nickel beneath it, maybe he planned to make some sort of deal with you—get you to threaten the surface landowner, whoever that turned out to be, with mineral exploitation or sell the land for development. Think about it."

She drew a knife through a blob of mozzarella and the tomato beneath it and continued, "If Toby still refused to sell, you could wave those mineral rights in his face and tell him if he doesn't sell, you'll start mining that nickel. He wouldn't want the land crisscrossed with excavation equipment, would he?"

"That's quite a scenario. Why not just tell me that?" Heath stared at his plate, wondering why he'd ordered so much food when his appetite had deserted him.

"C'mon, Heath. Your father has reason to believe Dead Falls Island is special to you. He must understand your hesitance with the idea of developing that property to dovetail with the casino."

"I guess he does." He jabbed at the pile of french fries on his plate with his fork. "You're not going to want half of these again like last night, are you?"

"I did *not* eat half of those fries last night, and no. I don't want anything greasy in my stomach for the flight home." She swirled her drink, causing more bubbles to fizz to the top. "Are you going to call him? Your dad."

"I'll try. He's on vacation in Italy with his new wife, who's a few years older than me, by the way."

"Hey, you can't hold that against the guy. Do you think he'll talk to you?"

"Depends on what kind of voicemail I leave him. If I come on strong, he'll put me on Ignore until he returns. But all of this, my ownership of the mineral rights and my father's knowledge of them, still doesn't explain why someone is targeting you."

"I think someone else knows about the nickel vein on Toby's land, but they don't know who owns it. Maybe that's what they were searching for the first time they broke into my place. The intruders searched an old suitcase that held my father's papers. I don't know if they found anything there or took anything, but maybe the fire was a way to make sure I didn't find anything, either."

"Or the fire was another warning. At least both of those incidents weren't a direct physical threat against you. You were out both times, but the poor dogs suffered."

She tossed back the rest of her mimosa. "I guess I should feel grateful that someone's not trying to kill me...like Toby." Willow raised a finger to the waitress and ordered another mimosa.

"We don't know that yet. I'm not sure what's taking the medical examiner so long to come to a determination. It would help if we knew whether your stalker is capable of murder." He spread his hands. "I mean, I'd go to greater measures to protect you."

She raised one eyebrow at him as he felt his face warm. She asked, "Now he's my stalker?"

"Or she." Heath sprinkled some vinegar on a piece of fish. "Ellie Keel is not happy with you."

"Wait until she finds out *you* own the mineral rights to her uncle's former property. She'll go ballistic."

"Can't wait for that. She and her brother will probably show up to this meeting with the Samish committee for the casino." He crunched into his fish.

"When is that? I got the notice but wasn't planning on attending. Maybe I should."

"You're a major player. The meeting is tonight at the Samish reservation. I'm supposed to present my progress with the adjacent land lots—yours and...yours now. We're opening the floor to dissent."

"I'm going to be even more well-liked than I already am around here." She smiled as the waitress delivered her second champagne flute.

"Are you sure that's the way to deal with your fear of flying?" He tapped the stem of her glass with his finger.

"I don't have a fear of flying regular commercial jets. Those puddle jumpers make me nervous. Flew one over the Cascades once, and I swear the engine sputtered." She shivered and took a generous sip of her drink. "Believe me. This will help for the ride back."

"I think you have more to fear from that meeting."

"I think *you* have more to fear from that meeting than I do." She picked up a piece of basil from her plate with her fingertips and dropped it into her mouth. "Are you going to come out against your own proposal at the meeting?"

"Nope. I'm just going to facilitate. I'm also not going to tell them about the nickel on Toby's property or the fact that I own the rights." Heath finished one piece of fish and eyed the other with distaste. He had knots in his stomach, too, but not from fear of flying.

"Oho, so you're throwing me to the wolves on my own, huh?" She dug her elbows into the table on either side of her plate. "You're going to point the finger at me as the baddie who won't sell."

"Nobody's going to be pointing any fingers. Everyone will have a chance to make their case. If you don't want to go, that's fine. Most people don't expect you to be there anyway. It was always Toby's property that was in play. Nobody ever expected you to sell."

"Unless I'm dead." Willow crossed her arms over her midsection. "Jason Hart suggested I make a will—and he wasn't kidding."

"If you died intestate, your mother would probably inherit. She's your closest relative." Heath tossed his napkin on his plate and finished his beer. "How does she feel about the property?"

Willow's green eyes sparkled as they widened. "You've been thinking about my death? Have it all figured out?"

"I confess. I did work it out in my head, but only for logistical reasons—kind of like Jason did." He grabbed her hand and kissed the inside of her wrist. "It might be what we're dealing with. That's why I want to keep you in my sights."

She didn't pull away, instead curling her fingers around his hand. "To answer your question, my mother hates Dead Falls Island. I'm pretty sure she'd sell that land in a second to fund her vagabond lifestyle. No doubt."

Squeezing her fingers, he said, "Don't tell anyone that."

"Question for you." She ran her fingertips along the length of his hand, giving him the shivers. "Are you going to continue digging? Do you still think Toby was telling the truth about your mom, or was it his way of messing with your mind?"

"I'll keep digging. I don't know what the man was up to, but I can't give up on my mother." He pulled out his wallet and snapped a credit card onto the table. "If it's okay with you."

"Paying or digging?"

He snorted. "I'm paying for lunch. I meant the digging."

"As long as you let me help you."

"Even with people shooting at us?"

"Maybe one of us can be the lookout while the other digs." She wiggled her fingers at the waitress.

"Another mimosa?"

"I wish." Willow winked at Heath. "Just the check."

Before the waitress turned away, Heath handed her his card. "Hopefully, Captain Mark hasn't spent his time on the island downing mimosas."

"He didn't look like the mimosa type." She wiped her hands on a napkin. "Is it time already?"

"We got what we came for—and then some." He paid the bill, and he and Willow decided to walk along the harbor on their way back to the airport.

They ran into their pilot coming out of a pizza place, a square box in his hand. He held up the box. "Leftovers. I can't offer meal service on my Cessna, but you can have it."

Heath answered, "We just had lunch, thanks."

"Did you get your business done?" Mark fell in beside them.

"We did." Heath gave a sharp nod. A slight pounding beat against his temples every time he thought about his father and his deception.

"How often do you make this flight?" Willow tripped over a bump in the sidewalk and grabbed on to Heath's arm.

"This island? A few times a week. More to the mainland. Private is more expensive than the airlines, but you can schedule at any time."

When they reached the small airport that consisted of a tower, a low-lying building, a couple of vending machines and the airstrip, Mark waved to some benches outside. "Hang out here for a few minutes. I need to go inside to file my flight plan."

Five minutes later, Mark emerged from the building pressing a bottle of water against his forehead. "Does it feel hot to you?"

"I'm a little warm." Heath tugged on his light windbreaker.

Mark performed some preflight checks before ushering them onto the plane again. They snapped in and grabbed their headsets. Mark spoke into the mic, and the plane's engines whirred to life. It made a slight turn, picked up speed, and soon after the island dropped away beneath them.

Willow closed her eyes, and Heath rested his forehead against the vibrating window to stare into the bay. Both he and Willow would have to make it clear to all interested parties, including his father, that if the Samish casino went ahead, it would do so without the adjoining land for additional facilities. If the Samish could still make that work, more power to them.

The airplane, which had been climbing, seemed to level off, and Heath glanced back at San Juan, still a visible chunk of land in the bay. Maybe the pilot was going to fly at a lower altitude on the way back, because this didn't seem like cruising.

The wing outside his window dipped to the right, and the plane veered slightly. Were they going back?

Heath tapped his headset. "Mark? Is there a problem?"

Captain Mark didn't respond, and Heath yanked off the headset. Maybe it wasn't meant to communicate to the pilot. He cupped a hand around his mouth and shouted, "Mark? Mark, are we going back?"

The pilot hadn't heard him, so Heath leaned into the aisle to get a clear view of the cockpit. As he did so, the nose of the plane dipped. "Mark!"

Mark didn't turn around or acknowledge him, and the plane had started losing altitude. The sound of the wind outside changed as the craft listed to the right.

Heath scrambled out of his seat, glancing over at Willow, still dozing in a champagne haze. In two long strides, he reached the cockpit and grabbed Mark's shoulder.

The pilot groaned and slumped to the side. Captain Mark was out cold.

Chapter Thirteen

Willow jerked awake. Had they landed already? She glanced across the aisle at Heath and jolted upright when her gaze met an empty seat. The plane dipped, and she dug her fingernails into the arm of her seat. Where the hell was Heath?

Cocking her head to the side, she checked the aisle, and her heart stopped when she saw Captain Mark on the floor, his legs in the cockpit and his torso extending into the aisle. With shaking hands, she clawed at the seat belt around her lap.

As she stood up, the airplane shuddered, and she yelped, making a grab for the headrest on the seat in front of her. Her knees trembled when she took a few unsteady steps toward the cockpit and the prone body of Mark.

"Willow?" Heath waved his hand in the air from the pilot's seat in the front. "Sit down and strap in. It's going to be okay."

"Okay? The pilot's dead."

"Mark's not dead. He can't fly, but I can. I have my pilot's license, and although it's been a few years, I can handle this craft. I'll get us down safely. Sit back down and breathe. I've already radioed ahead."

Willow shuffled back to her seat, dipping her head

to look out the window. Sky met blue water, with not a speck of dry land in sight. Swallowing hard, she dropped back down and snapped the belt, pulling it securely. She braced her forehead against the seat in front of her and murmured a prayer. She had to trust Heath—again.

She balled her hands into fists and buried them in her lap. Squeezing her eyes closed, she kept Heath's advice at the forefront, breathing in through her nose and exhaling through her mouth. The rhythm calmed her, as did the leveling out of the airplane.

Heath seemed to have gotten the situation under control, and the plane had stopped dipping and swaying. What would've happened if Heath didn't know how to fly? And what was wrong with Mark? He'd come out of the pizza place but didn't seem as if he'd been drinking.

After what felt like an eternity, the plane started to descend—in a good way. Willow finally lifted her head, hearing voices from the cockpit. That had to be a good sign.

Heath thrust his thumb in the air. "Coming in for a landing, Willow. I got this."

The plane dropped through the low clouds, turning Willow's world a misty gray. She licked her lips, ignoring the buzzing in her ears. The force of the descent pushed her back against the seat, and she held her breath as the plane wobbled.

She sneaked a peek out the window. Between the wisps of clouds skittering by, she spied the small runway on Dead Falls Island. A lone ambulance waited on the tarmac, its red light a beacon of safety. Was it there in case they crashed, or was it for Captain Mark?

A few minutes later the plane whooshed, and her

stomach dropped. When the wheels touched the ground, she let out a long breath on the tail end of a sob.

When the plane came to a complete halt, she jumped from her seat and made a beeline for the cockpit, where Heath was still flipping switches. She wanted to throw herself in his arms in gratitude and relief, but she dropped to the floor to check Mark's pulse instead. It beat slowly but steadily beneath her fingertips.

She put her face close to his and sniffed the breath huffing from his parted lips. The only alcohol she smelled was the champagne on her own breath.

Heath peeled himself out of the pilot's seat and knelt across from her on the other side of Mark. "Is he all right?"

"Sleeping like a baby. I don't understand."

He reached for her and cupped her jaw. "Are *you* all right?"

"I am now, thanks to you. What other hidden talents do you have?"

He quirked his eyebrows. "Stick around and find out, kid."

The shouting from outside the plane broke the tension between them, and Heath rose to his feet and stepped over Mark's prone form. He opened the door to a clutch of people, all hovering around the plane.

He jerked his thumb over his shoulder. "The pilot, Mark Santos, is on the floor. When I saw what was happening, I eased him out of his seat and laid him flat so I could take his place. I have no idea what happened. He seems to be sleeping. He didn't cry out, foam at the mouth, clutch his chest. He just fell asleep at the controls."

Willow joined Heath at the door, gulping in the fresh

sea breeze. "And he's not drunk. Didn't appear drunk when we boarded, and I just sniffed his breath."

The EMT closest to the plane gestured for them to step outside. "We'll take it from here."

After the ambulance had whisked Mark away, and after a good forty-five minutes of answering questions, Willow finally got her wish. As she and Heath faced each other on the tarmac, he opened his arms to her, and she fell against his chest.

His heart beat strong and steady beneath her cheek. "It gives me the chills to think about what would've happened to us if you weren't a pilot."

"But I am, so don't dwell on it. We're safe. You're safe."

She nestled closer into his embrace. "Did the EMTs say anything about Mark? What caused his collapse?"

"Not to me. Just asked a bunch of questions, which I tried to answer the best I could." He took her by the shoulders and looked down into her face. "Do you think it's a coincidence that we wound up on a plane with a disabled pilot?"

The dread that had been twisting her gut tightened its grip. "I—I don't know. Are you saying my stalker has graduated to murder?"

"Maybe, and he's *my* stalker now, too. I was in the plane with you. Who would've benefited if that Cessna had plunged into the sea?"

A quick breeze gusted up from the bay, and Willow's teeth chattered.

"Are you in shock?" Heath draped an arm around her shoulders. "Let's get in my truck."

She hung on to Heath numbly as he led her to his vehicle. Of course Mark's condition hadn't been an accident. Someone knew what they'd just discovered about the mineral rights. Someone knew they were the two impediments that stood in the way of this great land development—benefiting Bradford and Son, certain factions of the Samish and even the Keels.

Heath helped her into his truck and then slid into the driver's side. He punched on the engine and tabbed a few buttons on the console. Heat rose from the leather seat, warming her thighs and backside.

"This feels nice." She allowed the heat to seep into her rigid muscles, but she couldn't allow herself to get too comfortable. "You asked who would benefit from my death? My mother. As you mentioned before, my mother is my natural heir. She would get that land if I died."

"You really think your mom would put out a hit on you?"

"Would your dad put a hit on you?"

Heath clenched the steering wheel, his knuckles pale. "My father is a lot of things, and we haven't always had the best relationship, but kill his only son for a land deal? No way."

"Same." She curled one leg beneath her. "My mom won't win any mother-of-the-year awards, but she's made a nice life for herself, and we're on good terms now. Not only is she not the killing type, she couldn't care less about this island."

"But you said she'd sell the land if she had the chance, take the money and run."

"Of course she would if it dropped into her lap. But she's not going to take any extreme measures to get it. I'm sure she doesn't even know the drama surrounding this land deal." She stopped and nibbled on the tip of her finger. Or did she?

Heath glanced in her direction. "What? Did you think of something else?"

"Just something my mom said earlier about having contacts on the island. She knew we had a new sheriff, so maybe she does keep tabs on what's going on here." Willow flicked back her hair. "No. She's not going to have me killed to get property on Dead Falls. That's absurd."

"Okay, so we've ruled out our respective parents as murderers. That just leaves a whole bunch of other people."

She said, "Before the meeting, I'm going to my cabin to sort through the mess to see what I can salvage. What are you going to do?"

"I'm going to dig—and I mean that literally."

Wagging her finger in the air, she said, "You're supposed to wait for me."

"Let's do this. We'll regroup at the hotel, swing by your cabin to check it out and then head to Toby's cabin to resume digging."

"Okay. Can we squeeze in a visit to the dogs at Astrid's?" She put her hands together. "I don't want them to think I abandoned them."

"Meeting's at seven. I think we can do it." He gunned his engine. "Let's face the people trying to kill us."

WHEN THEY GOT back to the hotel, Heath retreated to his own room and fell across the bed. He couldn't decide what shocked him more—learning that his father already knew he owned the mineral rights to Toby Keel's property or discovering Captain Mark passed out in the pilot's chair on the Cessna.

Unseeing, he stared at the ceiling. He'd done his best to play it cool around Willow, but he'd been terrified flying that plane. He didn't know if Mark was dead behind him, or if something had been released in the Cessna and he and Willow would be the next ones to collapse. The act of flying had come back to him quickly, even though it had been a few years since he'd piloted a plane on his own.

The weather and course had been his friends today. If they'd had a longer flight or poor visibility, he didn't know if he could've flown and landed that craft safely.

And what the hell had happened to Mark? Nobody could tell him his mission on San Juan and Mark's incident were unrelated. He had to talk to Mark.

Rolling onto his stomach, he grabbed his phone and looked up the number for the hospital. He placed the call and explained to the nurse that he'd been with Mark Santos on the plane and wanted to speak with him.

The nurse wouldn't allow him to talk to Mark, who was resting, but she assured him the pilot would be fine and make a full recovery. She also wouldn't clue him in on what had caused Mark's collapse.

The police on the scene at the airport didn't seem overly invested in finding out what had happened to Mark. They saw it as an aviation issue and under their investigation. That agency would most likely be interested in what and how much Mark was drinking before the flight, or if he had any medical conditions that would preclude him from flying.

Heath was more interested in where Mark went when

he was on the island and who he met. Someone knew he and Willow were headed over there, but Heath couldn't figure out how.

He gave up on the nurse and left a message on Mark's voicemail. If the hospital released him tomorrow or even the next day, Heath wanted to talk to him.

After he changed into a pair of grungy jeans and his hiking boots, Heath went down the hall to check on Willow. He barely tapped a second time when she swung open the door.

His gaze flicked over her outfit, a carbon copy of his own, only she looked a lot better in it than he did. "Ready?"

"Uh-huh. I checked with the fire department, and they told me I could go back inside the cabin. I mostly want to check for photos and my clothes. I can always go back to my place in Seattle to pick up more clothes for the rest of the summer, but I want to salvage what I can."

"And the suitcase that holds your father's papers, right?"

"Honestly—" she let the door slam behind her as she hitched a small backpack purse over one shoulder "—I didn't find anything of importance in there when I looked."

"You should still take it, if the fire didn't damage it."

"Do you think someone searched those papers for the mineral rights?"

He shrugged as he stabbed the call button for the elevator. "At least we know it wasn't my father. He already knew."

Once outside, they climbed into the truck, and Heath's

finger hovered over the control for the heated seats. "You want your seat heated?"

"No. I recovered, sort of." She clicked her seat belt. "Do you see why I don't like flying in those little death traps?"

"It's not every day your pilot passes out." He reached over and squeezed her knee, which was bouncing up and down. "I called the hospital to check on Mark. The nurse wouldn't give me much, but he's out of danger."

"Did you get the impression the deputy at the scene was eager to turn the investigation over to the FAA?"

"Yep. Not his fault, though. Did you want to be the one to explain to him how we went over to San Juan to look up mineral rights, and we suspected that someone was trying to kill us because of that by incapacitating our pilot?"

"No." She twirled an auburn lock of hair around her finger. "But maybe West would be interested in our theory. He, at least, has an idea of what we've been facing."

"I also believe he thinks Toby was murdered. Whether the ME will find for homicide or not, West has a strong suspicion. He would've treated the scene in a different manner if he was sure Toby's death was an accident."

"I agree, so why didn't you report the gunfire last night?"

"You know why. I don't want anyone to know I'm digging holes around Dead Falls Island, not even Sheriff Chandler."

With a later sunset, they didn't need electricity to see inside Willow's cabin. The fire had burned away one wall and portions of the roof, so the sunlight streamed through the openings, giving them a clear picture of the wreckage.

As they stood in the doorway, surveying the damage, Heath entwined his fingers with Willow's. "This is bad. I'm sorry."

A smile wobbled on her lips, and she dashed a tear from her cheek. "It's not my permanent residence, and I'd already gotten rid of most of the furniture from my childhood. At least the dogs are safe, and I have you to thank for that."

He withdrew a pair of gloves from his back pocket. "You wear these while you're mucking around. I'll get the bins from the back of the truck, and you can tell me what to load up."

It took them about an hour to wade through the mess to locate framed pictures, a few salvageable books, dog food and the majority of Willow's clothes, still hanging in the closet in her room.

Outside, she brought a pile of clothes to her nose and buried her face in it. "They don't even smell that bad. I think a good wash will get the smoky smell out of them."

"I'm going back for that suitcase under the bed. You never know." He left her sorting through her clothing and tromped to the bedroom in the back where she'd pointed out the suitcase before.

Crouching down, he grabbed the handle and pulled it from beneath the bed. He glanced over his shoulder once and flipped open the top. Paul Sands had left behind a bigger filing nightmare than Toby Keel. Who could find anything in this mess? But maybe that was the point.

"Are you done?" Willow called from the front door, or at least the space where the front door used to function as a door.

"Coming." He heaved up the suitcase and lugged it

outside. "Why didn't anyone think of putting wheels on suitcases back then?"

"One of the mysteries of life." She shrugged. "Who files paperwork in a suitcase?"

When they finished loading the bins in his truck, Heath stood beside it, one hand on his hip. "Do we take the trail through the woods to Toby's, or should we drive around the bend and park near the other trailhead? I don't like the idea of leaving the truck with all your stuff in the back parked on the side of the road."

"Let's hike in. That way, we can see beforehand if anyone is skulking in the woods with a shotgun."

Their mode of transportation decided, Heath locked up his truck, and he and Willow ducked onto the trail that led to the other property. He carried the shovel and pickax with him. Willow assured him she'd found a shovel on Toby's property and had left it there when the shot rang out.

She said, "I can use that to dig."

He shifted the pickax from one shoulder to the other. "You don't have to dig. Just keep a lookout. Too bad we don't have the dogs with us."

"Exactly. We should've picked up the dogs first."

They emerged into the clearing for Toby's cabin, and Heath's gaze darted around the property. The yellow crime scene tape was even more bedraggled than the previous time he was here, and they still didn't even know if a crime had been committed or not.

He circled around the back of the cabin, and Willow followed him. He dropped his tools near the holes in the ground that he'd dug earlier and that Willow had enlarged. Pointing at the cabin, he said, "Why don't you go inside and look around some more? I'd feel better if you were inside instead of out here in the open."

"What am I looking for?"

He pulled on his gloves. "More documents, maybe some hiding places. Toby was a man with secrets."

"Okay, I'll pretend to be busy while you dig out here. Don't forget. I want to stop off at Astrid's to see the dogs before that meeting."

"I'll be quick." He clapped his hands together, dislodging some particles of dirt from the gloves. "I have a strange feeling about this place."

Heath breathed easier when he heard the cabin door close. Then he got to work. He hadn't been exaggerating to Willow about sensing something about this location. He'd felt it the first night he'd come to this cabin, winding up behind it instead of at the front door. An eerie sensation had made the hair on the back of his neck stand up and quiver. Willow's scream had punctuated that feeling, and finding Toby's body had convinced him that his original unease had been some kind of premonition about the man's death on the other side of the cabin.

Now that he knew this was the location that matched Toby's note, the feeling was back stronger than ever. That conviction gave strength to his efforts, and he plunged the shovel into the earth over and over.

After about an hour of work, during which Willow called out to him a few times and brought him a bottle of water, Heath leaned on the handle of the shovel. He wiped the sweat from his brow with the sleeve of his shirt. He'd made progress, but it would help if he actually knew what he was looking for.

He slid the shovel down the side of one of the ditches

and heard a rustling noise. He aimed his flashlight into the hole and saw the edge of something blue. Scraping the point of the shovel across the area revealed a larger swath of what looked like a blue-and-yellow rug. With his heart galloping in his chest, he raked the tip of his shovel across the object, removing more dirt and exposing more of the thick, rolled-up rug.

He dropped to the ground, lying flat on his belly, his head dipping into the ditch. The beam of his flashlight swept back and forth across the rug as he stretched his arm to reach it. Using his fingers, he sifted through some clods and rocks in the dirt until he met a long, smooth object.

He scrabbled in the dirt to free the item. Closing his fingers around it, he pulled himself from the hole.

Sitting back on his heels, he unfurled his hand. He gaped at the bone in his palm and released an anguished roar.

Chapter Fourteen

A strangled cry from outside assaulted her ears, and Willow clutched the notebook of recipes she'd found under a floorboard beneath Toby's bed to her chest. She scrambled to her feet and tore out of the cabin, stumbling down the porch steps.

"Heath?" She dropped the notebook as she careened around the corner of the cabin. Relief made her knees weak when she saw Heath crouched next to a ditch, the one he'd been working on the last time she came outside. *He hasn't been shot.*

Scooping in a breath, she charged toward him. "Heath!"

He slowly lifted his head and cranked it toward her like an automaton. His eyes blinked, and he held out his open hand toward her. "I found this. There's more."

She sank to the ground beside him and held out her hand. "What is it?"

Cupping his hand over hers, he dumped his find into her palm. "It's a bone. A human bone."

Willow examined the piece of bone, running a thumb along its concave surface. "I-it looks like a metatarsal bone—from a foot, but I can't tell if it's human. We don't know if it's from a human being."

"Do you know many animals out here that have metatarsal bones?"

"Deer, goats, pigs." She ran a tongue around her dry mouth.

"This long?" He jabbed a finger into the ditch. "And who wraps a dead deer in a rug?"

Willow clambered to the edge of the ditch on her hands and knees and peered into the darkness. It didn't remain dark for long as Heath lit up the area with his flashlight.

Her gut churned when she spotted the rolled-up rug at the bottom of the hole. Shaking her head, she choked. "You can't really believe this is…"

"My mother?" Heath clutched his hair with his dirty hand, and the grime streaked down his sweaty face. "Why else would Toby Keel direct me to this spot? He flat out told me that I could find my mother where the mist meets the earth between two giant maples. And here she is."

"Why? Why?" Willow clutched the base of her throat. "What does this even mean?"

"I'm heading back to the road to call the sheriff. Don't touch anything else." Rising to his feet, he stretched out a hand to her. "In fact, leave it. You're coming with me. I don't want you out here by yourself."

She waved vaguely at the buried rug. "Whoever killed this person—and I'm not convinced it's your mother—is long gone. I think I'm safe."

"Willow, you're not safe." He grabbed her hand and practically yanked her to her feet.

He kept a hold on her until they reached the trail that led to the road on the other side of Toby's property. Then they went single file while he literally watched her back.

She kept her phone out, waiting for a decent signal, and several yards before they hit the road, she got it. "I'm calling the sheriff's department right now."

She talked while she followed Heath onto the road. It took her a few minutes to explain to the sergeant at the desk that they had discovered bones and not a dead body. Once she made that clear, the sergeant's urgency level went down.

Willow rolled her eyes at Heath as he herded her into a turnout. "It's not an animal. The bones are wrapped in a blue carpet. Just tell Sheriff Chandler that the body... bones were found on Toby Keel's property, about twenty feet from where he died."

When she ended the call, she said, "I think I finally got through to him. Mentioning the sheriff helped."

Heath paced back and forth a few steps. "I don't know what this means. Did Toby murder my mother? If he'd just found her body after a suicide, why not report it? Why bury it?"

"Slow down." She rubbed a circle on his back. "We don't even know if that's your mother. Hell, we don't really know if the bones belong to a human. I just bluffed it with the sergeant so he'd get someone out here."

"Are they coming this way?" He jerked his thumb down the empty road.

"Yes. It's always easier to get to Toby's property from this direction."

"You don't have to wait." He glanced at his phone. "I know you want to see the dogs before the meeting tonight."

"Meeting is still on?" She raised her eyebrows. Heath

seemed too shaken right now to conduct a contentious meeting of warring parties.

"Now more than ever. I'm going to announce this development at the meeting and watch what happens."

His jaw tightened, and Willow revised her previous judgment of his emotions. Heath Bradford was determined... and maybe a little mad. Betrayed by his father. Betrayed by Toby. Maybe even betrayed by his mother.

"I'll stay with you. The dogs can wait. Astrid and Olly are spoiling them, from all accounts, and Sherlock likes having more canines in the house." She tucked her hand through the crook of his arm. She didn't want to leave him alone.

He trailed a finger across her cheek and tucked a strand of hair behind her ear. "Thanks."

Several minutes later, Sheriff Chandler himself pulled up in his SUV. He exited his vehicle, shaking his head. "What the hell is going on out here?"

"That's what we'd like to know." Heath strode forward and clenched the sheriff's hand. "Now would be a good time to know if Toby's death was a homicide."

"I can tell you—it's not going in that direction. The ME is stalled on undetermined. Toby had a heart attack. Whether he had it and fell, hitting his head, or when someone knocked him on the head is unclear." He stabbed a finger toward the woods. "How did you happen to come upon a set of buried bones?"

"I dug them up." Heath widened his stance and crossed his arms, as if expecting a physical challenge from West.

West scratched his chin. "Why were you digging on the property?"

"I own the mineral rights beneath the land."

West kept his face impassive, his only reaction the flaring of his nostrils. "So you decided to dig for the gold yourself?"

"Nickel." Heath drummed his fingers against his biceps. "Just curious."

"And instead of nickel, you found human bones wrapped in a rug."

"That's right."

Tipping his head in Heath's direction, West asked Willow, "You're okay with this guy digging trenches in your property to hunt for nickel?"

"We were both curious, West. Now we're even more curious. How are you going to handle this?"

"I'll have a look first, but we'll most likely cordon off the location until we can get some CSI folks from Seattle. We don't have the capability in our small lab to test bones, date them, determine a cause of death." He blew out a long breath. "I have a squad car on the way. Take me to your newest discovery. This is like déjà vu."

In a scene that was eerily familiar, the three of them tromped down the trail to Toby's cabin. When they got to the clearing and circled to the back of the cabin, West whistled through his teeth.

"Looks like you two have been busy." The sheriff crouched beside the ditch and aimed his flashlight at the rug below. "You took a bone out?"

In a macabre gesture, Heath pulled on his gloves and dug the foot bone from his front pocket. He held it up for West's scrutiny.

West swore under his breath and shook out a plastic bag from his pocket. "Drop it in here."

Heath complied and drew back as West pulled on his

own gloves and stretched out on the ground, his head poked below the earth. He shimmied forward until his midsection aligned with the edge of the trench, and then bent forward, the top half of his body disappearing.

Muffled curses reached them on the surface. When he scrambled out, the front of his uniform plastered with mud, he said, "There's a human skull in there."

Shouting from the woods had them all turning their heads, and West clambered to his feet. "Those are my deputies. They're probably lost. I'll be right back."

Looking at Heath's pale face, Willow swallowed. "It *is* human."

Heath glanced at the sheriff's retreating back and dropped to his knees next to the ditch. Mimicking West's position, he vanished into the ground as if being swallowed.

"Heath, what are you doing?"

He didn't answer her, and soon his legs dropped into the hole, too.

"West is not going to like this. You'd better get out before he…"

"Where's Heath?" West came charging back to the scene, a male and a female deputy trailing after him.

Heath's head popped up, dirt smudging his cheeks and sprinkled in his hair. "Sorry. I was having a look, and I fell in." He held up his gloved hands. "I'm wearing gloves, but I didn't touch anything anyway."

"Get out so we can secure this area. I already put a call in to Seattle, and they're going to bring equipment out here tonight so they can excavate the skeletal remains. They don't even want me or my people to touch anything."

"It's all yours." Heath hoisted himself from the grave and clapped his hands together, showering dirt to the ground. "We have a meeting to get to."

"How many more secrets can this island harbor?" West clasped the back of his neck and squeezed it. "That skull looks smallish. I'm hoping this is not another forgotten victim of Dr. Summers's killing spree of young boys several years ago."

"I-it's not a child." Willow twisted her fingers in front of her. If it were a child's skeletal remains, it couldn't be Jessica Bradford, Heath's mother, in there, but how awful it would be if this were another casualty of the sick obsession of Dr. Summers, a serial killer who'd targeted young boys on the island over the course of several years.

"I don't think so, but I'm not sure. That's why we have the experts coming out to excavate and transport the bones to a lab." West sidled in front of the hole and puffed out his chest, as if he feared Heath would make another attempt to dive in. "You two should get to your meeting. I suppose this is going to get out, isn't it? It's Dead Falls Island."

Tugging off his dirt-stained gloves, Heath said, "I think it's important to let all the parties interested in this development know that a body has been discovered on one of the parcels. That could hold up development for quite a while, couldn't it, Sheriff?"

"I thought you *wanted* to develop these properties." West narrowed his eyes, and his gaze shifted from Heath to Willow. "Never mind. I'll keep you posted."

Heath snorted. "Like you're keeping us posted on Toby?"

Done with the two of them, West waved his hand in

the air and addressed the female deputy. "Amanda, can you start marking off this area?"

Willow grabbed Heath's arm. "Let's get out of here."

She made a detour to Toby's porch to scoop up the journal she'd found beneath the floorboards under his bed, rolled it up and shoved it in her pocket. She'd forgotten all about it when Heath yelled. Now it didn't seem that important compared to Heath's discovery.

Lost in their own thoughts on the trail, they didn't talk much on the way back to her burned-out shell of a cabin and the remains of that cabin stuffed in bins and waiting in the back of Heath's truck.

He smacked a hand on the tailgate. "Where are you going to put this stuff?"

"There are storage containers in town. I'll rent one until I figure out where I'm going to stay for the rest of the summer. It can't be that hotel. I'd never get any research done—not that I'm accomplishing much now."

"You're not going to be able to do it before the meeting."

"Are we going to be able to do anything before the meeting?" She brushed a hand down the front of his dirty shirt, and her fingers hit a round object stuck in the breast pocket.

He jerked back quickly and placed his hand over his heart as if to protect the object.

"What is that?"

He closed his eyes, and a muscle ticked at the corner of his mouth.

A breath hitched in her throat. She just wanted to take his face in her hands and kiss away that spot of throbbing tension. "Show me, Heath. I can't help you if you don't share with me. And I want to help you sort this out."

With his eyes still closed, he fished into his pocket with two fingers and withdrew a gold locket on a chain.

Willow watched the necklace glint in the setting sun, her breath coming in shallow gusts. "Where did you get that? What does it mean?"

"I found it amid that pile of bones wrapped in the rug and buried in the ground. It was my mother's."

Chapter Fifteen

Willow pressed her own hand against his empty pocket, over his heart. "You're sure?"

His eyes flew open, and he wedged a thumbnail in a crease in the locket, prying the two pieces apart. He cradled the open locket in his palm and held it out to her. "My picture and lock of my baby hair. She always wore it. Told me even though she couldn't always be present for me, she kept me close to her heart always."

Tears pricked the backs of Willow's eyes, blurring her view of the smiling baby and a lock of soft blond hair on the other side of the locket. She sniffed. "Heath, I'm so sorry. Why didn't you tell Sheriff Chandler?"

"I will." He snapped the locket shut. "I didn't want to get into it with him—how I knew to dig out there. What did I know about her death. I know nothing, but I'm going to find out one way or another."

Hooking two fingers in the front pocket of his jeans, she yanked him toward her. "I'll help. You know I will. I think it's all connected somehow—the properties, your mother, my father, Toby, the stalking and the attempts on our lives. We're looking at the obvious suspects—the people who want to develop the land—but maybe it's not all about the casino project."

He wedged a finger beneath her chin and tilted her head back. He brushed his lips with hers in a gentle kiss. "Thank you for being here. You're a lot like your dad in some respects. He was there for me, too, when Mom disappeared. Now you're here the moment I found her."

A chill zigzagged down Willow's spine at Heath's words. Jessica Bradford's death bracketed by two Sands family members didn't feel like a coincidence. It meant something, but she couldn't put her finger on it…not yet.

"And you'll be there for me at the meeting, too, right?" She tugged on the hem of her sweatshirt. "Not only do we not have time to visit the dogs, but we also don't have time to shower and change."

"I have some wipes in the car. Your clothes don't look bad. I was the one crawling in the dirt." He opened his shirt and shook it out, returning the locket to his breast pocket.

"It's only the outside." She stood on her tiptoes and grabbed the shoulders of his shirt, peeling it back. "I don't think anyone would care if you showed up to the meeting in a white T-shirt. I know I wouldn't mind."

He gave her a crooked smile as he caught the shirt and bunched his hand around the pocket. "Don't want to lose this."

"Absolutely not. Sorry." She held out her hand. "Let me put that in my purse, unless you want to leave it in your truck. You can't keep stuffing it into your pockets."

Heath retrieved the necklace and poured it into her hand, where it pooled in her palm. A sprinkling of goose bumps prickled across her arms as she closed her hand around a locket that had been buried with a dead woman for over ten years.

When they climbed into the truck, Heath pulled a container of wet wipes from the console and offered it to her. "It might be a little harsh on your face, but you only have a smudge of dirt on your chin, probably from my dirty hands."

She plucked a few wipes from the cylinder and scrubbed her hands. As she looked around for a bag for her trash, Heath said, "Turn this way."

She cranked her head to the side, and he dabbed her chin with the corner of a wipe. "There. I think I got it."

"Making me presentable for the drawing and quartering?"

"Any drawing and quartering is going to have to go through me first." He swiped the back of his neck with a towelette and reached into the back seat for a plastic bag. He dangled it from his fingers as he shook it up and down. "You can put your trash in here."

They finished cleaning up, and Heath started the truck. As he turned onto the road, Willow gathered her hair into a ponytail and clasped it over her shoulder. "Do you think Toby murdered your mother?"

"I have no idea. Why would he? But if he didn't, how would he know where she was...buried?" Heath flexed his fingers on the steering wheel.

"You said he told you they were close at the end, that she confided in him." She twisted her hair. "What if... what if he came on to her and she rebuffed him?"

Heath jerked his head toward her. "You mentioned that before. Do you really think that happened?"

"My mom implied Toby was a womanizer. Why would she lie?"

"That guy?" Gripping the steering wheel, Heath sat forward in the driver's seat. "Hard to believe."

"Why? Because he was something of a recluse? Perfect setting, actually. A lot of guys pretend to be a shoulder to cry on just to get close to a woman, gain her confidence, create an intimate emotional bond. Then bam."

"Bam. You mean he uses that to try to take the relationship to a different level, a physical level."

"Maybe your mom thought she had a friend, a confidant, and Toby wanted something more. Maybe he thought your mother was ripe for the picking and then easy to dispose of—" she clutched her throat "—sorry, because she had some mental health issues. Your father knew she had been suicidal in the past."

"You could be right, but why direct me to her grave? Especially me. If he had a guilty conscience after all these years, why not just turn himself in to the police?"

"He was ill, maybe sicker than anyone knew. It could've been the way he wanted to go out." Willow clasped her hands between her knees. "Do you think your mother's death has anything to do with the mineral rights on the property? Why did my father deed those to you? None of it makes sense."

"And why is it all important enough to want to kill two people?" He pointed his finger at her and then himself.

They continued asking each other almost rhetorical questions until Heath passed the stone sign indicating they'd crossed into the Samish reservation.

He made a few turns and tapped on the window. "The meeting is at the community center, and it looks like there's a standing-room-only turnout."

Willow took in all the cars parked at the side of the building and the line of people waiting to get inside. Her belly flip-flopped at the thought of being persona non grata at this event. She murmured, "Maybe I should've gone to Astrid's to visit the dogs. I would've been more welcome there."

"Don't worry." He threw the truck in Park and squeezed her knee. "I'm going to take all the heat off of you."

Placing her hand over his, she said, "Are you sure you're up to this, Heath? You just discovered that your mom is dead. We can leave right now, or you can leave, and I'll face them myself."

He killed the engine and released a long breath. "I always figured she was dead, so that part didn't hit me hard. I also suspected that Toby was sending me on a search for her body. Yeah, I admit actually finding her was a shock, but now I'm determined to figure out what happened to her and who's responsible. I may be way off, but this meeting is a starting point. All of this started when Bradford and Son agreed to partner with the Samish to develop the casino resort. They have to be connected."

"I agree, but you can hold this meeting another day."

"Really?" He slipped his hand from beneath hers and reached for the door. "Someone tried to kill us today, Willow. How much time do you think we have until they're successful?"

"Okay, let's do this." She pushed out of the truck and put her arms through the straps of her backpack purse.

As Heath took her arm to walk through the doors of the community center, Willow pinned back her shoulders and lifted her chin. The crowd parted for them, and she tuned out their chatter. As they ascended the dais that sported a long table, several chairs and a laptop connected to a projector, Willow caught the eye of Mindy Whitecotton, a Samish native, who worked at the university in Seattle.

Mindy gave her a wink, and the knots in Willow's gut loosened just a little.

Heath pulled out the chair in the middle, in front of the laptop, for Lee, and Willow slid into the chair on the end before Heath could get any crazy ideas and seat her next to Lee. An associate of Lee's sat next to him on the other side, and Willow flattened her lips when she saw Ellie Keel take the chair next to him.

As Heath lowered himself into the seat beside her, Willow nudged him with her elbow and hissed, "What's Ellie doing up here?"

"Maybe Lee invited her." Heath put his finger to his lips as Lee tapped the microphone.

"There should be room for everyone. There are a few empty seats in the front." He cupped his hand in the air. "Everyone is welcome. Everyone, come in."

Willow gazed at the stragglers squeezing past knees to grab lone seats. Lee must feel confident that he had majority support for the casino project. Garrett Keel raised his hand from his seat in the front row to wave at her, and she nodded back. Then she folded her hands in front of her as Lee started the presentation.

When the lights dimmed and the video started, Willow shifted her chair to see the plans for the new casino and the support facilities for it that would never be built on her property—no matter how many of her cabins burned down.

The video presentation ended, and a buzz of excitement rippled through the room. Maybe Heath should've led with the odds of this thing getting built before Lee drummed up the enthusiasm for it.

Lee smiled and rubbed his hands together. "Beautiful, isn't it? But we can't do it alone. That's why we're partnering with Bradford and Son. So let me introduce you to Heath Bradford, who spent some time here on the island with his family and never forgot its beauty and potential. Let's welcome Heath tonight."

A smattering of applause accompanied Heath as he stood up and took the mic from Lee. When it faded, he said, "Lee's right. The Samish need to partner with a developer, us, to realize the full extent of Lee's…vision. As he mentioned, the Samish have the land for a small casino on the leeward side of the island but will need more land to increase the profitability of the casino with adjacent hotels and restaurants."

Someone yelled from the back. "Do we have Toby's land now?"

"About that." Heath cleared his throat. "As I'm sure all of you know by now, Toby Keel passed away, and he owned one of the properties we were looking into acquiring."

Several people started chanting, "Ellie, Ellie, Ellie."

Ellie Keel jumped up from her seat and waved her arms as if she were at a political rally. She reached over the table and snatched the mic from Heath. "You all know my uncle died, but what you don't know is that he left the property to Willow Sands, the owner of the other property in question."

The room erupted, and Heath sidled behind Willow's

chair and placed a hand on her shoulder. Her hands still folded, Willow gazed out at the agitated crowd.

When they quieted down to a low hum, Ellie continued, "But just to let you know, my brother, Garrett, and I plan to sue to get the property in our names."

Mindy Whitecotton stood up and confronted Ellie. "You and Lee are just assuming all of us Samish want to exploit our land for profit. When did you hold the last vote, Lee? Where are those results? Where's the transparency regarding the support of this abuse of our land?"

More cries went up, and Willow couldn't tell where most people stood. She did mouth a silent thank-you to Mindy.

Heath rapped on the table to restore some order and asked Ellie for the mic, which she grudgingly handed over. "Look, this is an emotionally charged issue. The bottom line is the developers are not going to convince Willow Sands to sell out for this project. Ever. If the Keels are successful in their lawsuit, maybe we have room to move forward. However..." Heath stopped and inhaled, expanding his chest. "...there are new circumstances on Toby's former property that'll put a stop to any designs on that land."

Lee's head shot up. "What are you talking about, Heath?"

A muscle twitched at the corner of Heath's eye, and Willow longed to stand up, take the mic away from him and lead him out of here.

"Skeletal remains were found buried behind Toby's cabin."

The room descended into chaos again, and Willow had had enough. As several people surged toward the dais, smacking the table and shouting questions, she dragged her sweatshirt from the back of her chair. The notebook containing recipes, which she'd unearthed from Toby's cabin, fell onto the floor.

Willow picked it up and smoothed it out on the table, then hoisted her bag next to it. She stuffed the notebook inside the purse; she and Heath could have a look at it later, once she got him back to the hotel and they had a proper meal. She doubted Toby would bother hiding something that was just a homemade book of recipes.

The attendees began to dissipate, but Heath was still in an intense conversation with Lee.

Ellie planted herself in front of Willow. "Just what are you up to now? Are you going to make some sort of claim that the skeleton belongs to some long-lost Samish and that land is sacred burial ground? You do not get to appropriate our culture."

Willow ignored Ellie's finger stabbing at her because she couldn't drag her gaze away from the red flannel shirt draped over Ellie's arm. Was it missing a piece?

"Willow's not even the one making the claim, Ellie, and Heath didn't say anything about a burial place. It's probably another one of gruesome Dr. Summers's victims." Garrett draped an arm over Ellie's shoulder. "Let's go, sis, and maybe let go."

Willow watched them as they turned away and made for the exit, Ellie struggling to stuff her arms into the flannel shirt.

Heath finished his conversation with Lee, who was staying behind with a few helpers to gather their materials and straighten up the community center.

As they walked back to Heath's truck, Willow said,

"I saw Ellie wearing a red flannel tonight, and she sure came in with both barrels blazing."

Heath raised an eyebrow as he opened the passenger door. "I can't see Ellie skulking around the woods outside your cabin in her stiletto heels."

"People can change shoes."

When he settled next to her behind the wheel, he turned to her. "But you're right about her going off. Maybe she mentioned the lawsuit to see how many people are on her side."

"There were a lot in favor of the expanded casino, but there were plenty who seemed okay with the smaller effort or no effort at all, thanks to Mindy Whitecotton." She placed her purse on the floor between her feet. "Do you mind stopping by the storage facility in town? I talked to Levi, who owns the place, when you were digging. He booked a unit for me and said the attendant would be there until midnight. Said I could stop by anytime before then."

"That's fine. As long as you don't mind grabbing a bite to eat in town after we stash your stuff. I haven't eaten since we had that lunch before the plane drama."

"Do you know how Captain Mark is doing?"

"I haven't called again since the earlier call, but I'll try again tomorrow morning. I'd sure like to know what happened in that pizza place before our flight."

"I'm sure he wants to know what happened, too. His pilot's license is on the line if the FAA determines he knowingly drank or did drugs before flying."

As Heath navigated his truck back to town, Willow patted the bag at her feet. "During all the excitement, I forgot to tell you that I found a hiding place in Toby's cabin. I removed the only item that he stashed there."

"What did you find?"

She unzipped her purse and withdrew the notebook with pictures of fruits and vegetables on the cover. She waved it. "It looks like a recipe book. I thumbed through a few pages, and it's filled with handwritten recipes."

"Why would Toby be hiding a cookbook?" He pulled up to the last stop sign before heading into town and glanced at the notebook in her hand.

"No clue. Maybe he had other things stored there over the years, and this was just a leftover. It's odd that he hid it, though." She dropped the notebook on the floor next to her purse and pointed out the window. "Take that turn up there."

She continued giving him directions to the storage containers until he pulled up to the boxy building that sat just outside a locked gate. The glow from the office highlighted a man sitting at a desk.

"He must be the night clerk. I'll jump out and get my key."

Heath pulled in front of the office, and Willow hopped from the truck, dragging her purse with her.

After some exchange of information, Willow grasped the key to her unit and returned to the truck. The gate slid open, and Heath rolled through.

Less than thirty minutes later, her boxes and bins neatly lining the interior of the storage unit, they pulled away from the facility amid a discussion about what to eat.

Heath's preference for bar food won out, so they meandered to the Salty Crab, which boasted a rambunctious crowd long past the dinner phase of their evening.

With most of the clientele watching a game at the bar or playing pool in the back, Heath and Willow snagged a table by the window.

They ordered beers and a variety of appetizers. When the beers arrived, Heath took a long pull from his. "I can't believe the day we had. I feel like we're on a runaway train heading for some catastrophe."

"You and me both." She ran a thumb up the side of her sweating bottle. "The only good thing about this summer is…you."

"I feel the same way. I had such a thing for you back in the day. I even blurted it out to your father."

"Really?" Her face warmed beneath his intent stare, and she wrinkled her nose. "He never mentioned it to me."

He snapped his fingers. "Hey, maybe that's why he left the mineral rights to me and the property to you— so we'd be joined forever."

"It's as good a guess as any." She ran the tip of her finger around the rim of her bottle. "He should've told me. Maybe we could've at least gotten to know each other better."

"We're doing that now, aren't we?"

"Yeah, but it feels…" She lifted her shoulders. "…I don't know…forced, like we almost don't have a choice in the matter."

"Like it's part of that runaway train?" He moved his bottle out of the way to make room for the waitress to put down several plates of deep-fried junk food.

"A little." She pinched a hot onion ring between the tips of her fingers and waved it in the air. "Not to say I'm not fully in charge of my faculties and making decisions on my own."

"I would be surprised if you ever made a decision that wasn't wholly yours." He squirted a puddle of ketchup on the edge of one of the plates.

They concentrated on their food for several minutes, but Willow couldn't stay away from the subject at hand for long. She swiped a napkin across her mouth. "Were you ever able to reach your father and ask him why he didn't tell you about the mineral rights?"

"Nope." Heath crunched into a fried zucchini stick, which they'd ordered at her insistence.

"You're going to tell him about your mom, right?"

"Not immediately. I'll wait until the final identification has been made."

She tipped the rest of her beer into her mouth and grabbed her sweatshirt. "I'm going to use the ladies' room. Be right back."

He circled a finger at her sweatshirt as she shoved her arms in the sleeves and grabbed her purse. "You need a sweatshirt for the restroom?"

"It's out back. This is a high-class joint. Can't you tell?"

As she swept past him, he captured her hand and kissed it. The stupid smile on her face lasted until she pushed through the back door of the bar. The music faded as she crossed the alley to the public restrooms, shared by several businesses on this street.

She reached for the door handle, and a shadow appeared around the corner of the building. As she turned toward the source, she felt a sharp pain scream through her head.

She took a quick, gasping breath before the darkness enveloped her.

Chapter Sixteen

Heath swept the last onion ring through the smear of ketchup on his plate and popped it in his mouth. When the waitress appeared at the table to collect some plates, he stopped her. "Hey, where are the restrooms?"

"They're out the back door by the bar." She rolled her eyes. "We have to share public restrooms with the other businesses, but don't worry. They're all closed now, so those bathrooms are all ours."

"Thanks." Heath glanced at his phone, and a muscle twitched in his jaw. What was taking Willow so long?

He hailed the busy waitress again to tell her they hadn't left yet and to leave the check. Then he made a beeline to the back door. As he opened it, a woman crashed against his chest.

"Whoa, sorry..." he began.

She grabbed a handful of his shirt. "There's a woman by the bathrooms. She's on the ground, unconscious."

Adrenaline surged through Heath's body so fast, his head swam. "Go to the bar and get some help, and call 911."

As the woman stumbled toward the bar, Heath charged outside. The lights from the building illuminated Willow's still form on the ground. He rushed to her side and dropped to his knees.

"Willow! Willow!" As he brushed her hair from her face, his fingers met a sticky wetness.

She moaned, and relief swept through his body.

"Help is on the way. Don't try to move right now. You have a head injury. Does anything else hurt?" He ran his hands over her body and didn't feel any more blood.

The bartender ran outside and hovered over Heath with some towels. "Laila wasn't sure what happened, but she did see some blood. Use these."

Heath tugged a towel from the bartender's hand and pressed it against the spot on Willow's head where he'd seen the blood. "Did you call 911?"

"On the way. Does she need water?" The bartender held up a bottle.

Willow croaked out a few unintelligible words, and Heath put his ear to her mouth.

"Ambulance is on the way," he promised her. "You're gonna be fine."

She curled her fingers around his arm and rasped, "Help me sit up. I'm okay."

"Let's wait for the EMTs. Do you want some water?"

She answered, "Yeah, prop me up, and I'll drink some water."

Heath crawled behind her and hoisted her body half-way into his lap while holding the towel against her head.

Seeing Heath's struggle, the bartender crouched down and held the water bottle to Willow's lips. "Here you go. What happened out here?"

Willow swallowed most of the water, while some of it dribbled down her chin, mixing with the blood that had trickled down her face from her head wound. "I think someone hit me, like with an object on the side of my head. He came up behind me."

The bartender whistled. "That's messed up. Even more reason why we need our own bathroom inside the bar. Did he...assault you?"

"No!" Willow pushed away the water bottle and patted her shoulder and the ground next to her. "Where's my bag?"

Heath scanned the ground. "Your purse?"

"Yeah, the backpack purse I was wearing when I walked out here. At least I had my phone in my pocket." She grimaced and squeezed her eyes closed.

"Don't worry about that now." Heath lifted his head. "I hear the sirens. Just relax."

"Relax?" Willow struggled against him but tired out after a few seconds. "I was just bashed on the head and mugged—for my purse. Why do they want my purse, Heath?"

The bartender scratched his head. "Uh, probably wanted your cards and cash, but you can cancel those cards. It's your head you need to worry about."

Her question confused the bartender, but Heath knew exactly what she meant. This mugging was all part of what they were discovering about his mother, the nickel vein, the properties, the development plan.

When the ambulance arrived, it dispersed the small crowd of people who had gathered in the alley to watch the drama. The EMTs fussed over Willow and walked her to the back of the ambulance while Heath talked to the deputy who'd come out on the call.

"Deputy Fletcher." He shook Heath's hand. "I'll talk

to Willow once she gets sorted out over there, but you said she didn't get a look at her attacker?"

"Saw his shadow, and while she turned, he hit her. Stole her purse."

"You wouldn't happen to know what her purse looks like, would you?" Deputy Fletcher scratched a few notes on his pad.

"It was one of those purses that doubles as a backpack, so kind of big, but I couldn't tell you the color." Heath shrugged. "The purse may have just been a cover. Willow's cabin was ransacked, and then someone set it on fire. This has to be connected to those events."

"Doesn't sound like someone's trying to kill her. He could've finished the job here. You think it's some kind of scare tactic to get her to sell that property for the casino?"

"Sounds like you already know a lot, but not everything." Heath twisted the towel stained with Willow's blood in his hands. "There was an incident on a small plane we hired to San Juan. The pilot collapsed."

Fletcher bounced his pencil on the notepad. "I heard about that. That was you? You have your pilot's license? I'm taking flying lessons right now."

"That's great, but the point is Willow could've died if that plane had crashed, so I'm sure this is more than a run-of-the-mill mugging."

"It might be, but we have no witnesses, no description from Willow, no cameras, no weapon." Fletcher tipped his head toward Willow, sitting on the back of the ambulance, a white bandage on her head. "I'll ask Willow a few questions."

As Fletcher questioned Willow, Heath stopped one

of the EMTs. "Is she going to be okay? What happened to her?"

The EMT tapped his head. "Someone hit her on the side of the noggin with a blunt object. Piece of wood, maybe. Found some slivers in her hair. She'll be fine. Doesn't want to go to the emergency room and doesn't need to. Shouldn't be driving or be on her own tonight, just in case she shows signs of a concussion."

"I'll take care of her. Pain meds?"

"Ibuprofen in another four hours, if she needs it."

The deputy and the EMTs wrapped up about the same time, and Heath and Willow watched them leave from the back door of the bar. He took her hand. "I shouldn't have let you come out here on your own."

"Nonsense. It's a well-lit alley to the bathrooms. Whoever hit me knew we were here and was waiting for an opportunity. He saw it and grabbed it." She tilted her head and fingered her bandage.

"What is it? Do you remember something?"

"Perfume. I smelled perfume before I got whacked. What if it is Ellie? Did you see her tonight? She was livid."

"The perfume could've come from anywhere. Lots of women crossing back and forth in that alley." Noticing the set of her jaw, Heath said, "But we can have West talk to her. Maybe if she suspects we're onto her, she'll back off."

"Why did they take my purse?"

"Like I told Deputy Fletcher, the purse could've just been a ruse to make it look like a mugging in their continuing plan to terrorize you."

"It's all so senseless. After what you sprang on everyone tonight, you'd think they'd just leave this alone for a while." She ran a tongue along her bottom lip. "I'm dying of thirst. Can we go back inside and get something to drink?"

"When I left, I told the waitress we weren't skipping out on the check and to leave it on the table. It's probably still there."

They shuffled back into the Salty Crab, and several people peppered them with questions and offered their condolences. Their table still sported Willow's half-full beer bottle and a pair of bedraggled chicken wings, but no check.

Heath went to the bar to get Willow a Coke. He gave the bartender a fist bump. "Thanks for your help out there, man. You can send the waitress over with our check and add a couple of Cokes to it."

The bartender waved a tattooed arm. "On the house, my man. Hope Willow's okay."

A few minutes later, Heath carried the drinks back to the table where Willow was scrolling through her phone. He put her drink down on a coaster. "Too bad your phone wasn't in your purse. At least we'd have a way to track it."

"Not if they turned the phone off immediately. Then I would've been out a purse *and* my phone." She smacked the table. "My key. The key to my new storage unit. Maybe they followed us there and wanted to search my unit. See what I rescued from the fire."

"I didn't think of that, but the storage facility has cameras. They can't just waltz in there, even with a key."

"Ever hear of disguises? And I had a security camera at my place. Didn't stop someone from burning it down." She sucked down her drink with the straw. "Let's go back to the storage facility."

"Now?" Heath settled back in his chair and crossed his arms. "What do you expect to find there at this hour?"

"Um, someone using my key to get into my storage unit. I still even had the card in my purse with my unit number." Willow was already halfway out of her seat.

Heath gulped down the rest of his drink and followed her. So much for taking care of Willow.

He drove back to the storage facility, with the same attendant in the tiny office. "I'll go in with you this time."

The man in the office buzzed the door open when he spotted Willow out the window. As they entered, he said, "More to load up? Hey, what happened to your head?"

"Hi, Zev." Willow patted her bandage. "Someone mugged me and stole my purse. The key to my unit was in there, along with the unit number, and I'm afraid whoever stole it is planning to come here and rip me off."

"That's not cool. Nobody has been here this evening since you left, but that key opens the gate to the entire facility. They could come after hours."

Heath rubbed Willow's back. "We can't spend all night out here, keeping watch. You need to get some rest."

Zev spread his hands. "We have cameras, if that helps."

"Someone could come in here with a disguise—a hoodie, a face mask—we wouldn't know who it was." Willow sagged against the desk, her face pale.

"Okay, that's it. You're going back to the hotel now." As Heath curled an arm around Willow's waist, he asked

Zev, "Is there something you can do to prevent the mugger from getting in?"

"I'll tell you what." Zev clicked on his keyboard. "I'm going to assign you a different unit right now. You didn't have much stuff, did you? I'll bring a forklift to your unit and move the contents tonight. If this mugger does come back here, he's gonna find an empty unit. Will that work?"

"But we won't be able to catch them in the act."

Heath placed a finger against Willow's trembling lips. "It'll work for now. Thanks, Zev. We'll pick up her new key tomorrow morning."

They left the unit, and Willow collapsed in his truck. "I'm exhausted."

"Of course you are. I'm running on empty here, and I didn't even get bashed on the head." As he backed out of the parking space in front of the storage facility, Willow's phone buzzed.

"Don't answer that."

She glanced at the display. "It's the DFSD. Hello?" She listened for a few seconds and said, "We'll be right there."

Heath groaned. "What wild-goose chase are we going on now?"

"Someone found my purse down by the harbor and turned it in to the sheriff's department. Maybe they snagged my storage unit key and didn't want to be caught with the purse."

"This is it. The last stop of the day." Heath peeled out of the parking lot and barely stayed within the speed limit on his way to the DFSD.

Deputy Fletcher met them in the lobby. "Good news, huh? I was just getting ready to go off duty when a couple who was spending the night on their boat came in. Found it right by the dock. And your credit cards are still in there, although I do recommend you replace them just in case. Oh, and if you had any cash, that's gone."

Willow thrust out her hand. "Give it over."

Fletcher's eyebrows jumped to his hairline. "Sure, it's behind the desk. Sarge?"

An officer on the phone reached beneath the counter and handed Willow's purse to Fletcher. Willow practically snatched the purse from his hand and carried it to the seats against the wall.

She unzipped the bag and turned it upside down, shaking out the contents onto one of the chairs. Her wallet dropped out, along with a small makeup bag, a sunglasses case, a few pens, some spare change and other odds and ends. Willow pounced on a silver key and held it up. "It's the storage unit key."

"I guess they weren't planning to search your unit after all." Heath crouched down to retrieve a couple of items that had rolled under the chair. "Don't forget these."

Willow stared at the objects in his palm and pinched a silver tube of lipstick between her fingers. "This isn't mine."

"It fell onto the floor from your purse."

She carried the lipstick in front of her as if it was dynamite and parked herself in front of Fletcher. "You said you checked my wallet for my cards. Did you see this lipstick when you did?"

"Oh, that. The couple who turned in your purse said the lipstick was a few feet away from the purse itself. They figured it had fallen out, along with a few coins that had rolled in that same direction. They just dropped it back into the purse."

"It's not mine."

Fletcher shrugged and turned away to finish his conversation with the sergeant, but Heath watched Willow's wide eyes.

"What's wrong, Willow?"

"The lipstick isn't mine, but maybe it belongs to the person who stole my bag." She pulled off the lid and cranked up the scarlet-red lipstick. "And I know who wears this shade."

Chapter Seventeen

Willow waved the lipstick in Heath's face. "It's hers. It belongs to Ellie Keel. She always wears this hideous shade—day or night."

Heath led her out of the station with a backward wave to the deputies. "Maybe it is Ellie's, but why? Why did she take your purse only to dump it? You found your storage unit key, so it's not that. You think she needed a couple of bucks that badly?"

"I don't know, Heath." Willow clutched the bag to her chest. "Maybe she copied the key. Maybe she took my hotel key." With shaky fingers, she unzipped the side pocket of the purse and felt for her hotel key card. She pulled it out. Tears sprang to her eyes, and she slid down the wall of the station into a crouching position.

"Are you all right?" Heath knelt before her on the ground.

"Physically, I'm fine. I'm just so frustrated. What does she want?"

"Physically, you're not fine. I'm taking you back to the hotel now, and I don't care if someone sets fire to your storage unit. We're not making any detours."

She gave in and gave herself over to Heath's tender

care. He helped her to her feet, dried the tears on her cheeks and half carried her to his truck.

When they got back to the hotel, Heath took her to her own room, but he followed her inside. "A warm bath, some hot tea, ibuprofen and rest. Dr. Heath's orders."

She managed a smile. "I like the sound of that."

"Sit." He maneuvered her to the bed and placed gentle pressure on her shoulders. "I'm going to run that bath and have a cup of tea waiting for you when you come out, unless you want something stronger. I'm not sure the EMTs would recommend alcohol for a concussion, though."

"I don't have a concussion, but tea sounds perfect."

She closed her eyes to the sounds of the water running in the tub. When Heath came out of the bathroom, he crouched in front of her and removed her shoes.

"Go relax. I'll make the tea and leave a message for West to look into Ellie Keel. We don't have much proof, but we have the lipstick. He can at least start talking to her."

Willow shuffled to the bathroom, peeled off her clothes and sank into the tub. What was Ellie looking for? Did the woman really believe that if Willow and Heath were out of the way, she could get Willow's mother to sell the property? What good would the casino development do her, even if Mom did sell? Ellie wouldn't get the money from that sale. She must have some other interests in the casino deal. Maybe she'd worked out something with Lee.

These thoughts were not helping her relax. She cupped warm water in her hands and tipped it onto her chest. She took deep breaths through her mouth and exhaled them from her nose. Her muscles still ached with tension, and the questions still buzzed through her brain.

There was only one person who could settle her mind and soothe her body. "Heath!"

He poked his head into the room as if he'd been waiting outside. "Yeah? You okay?"

"You were the one digging today. Don't you need a bath?"

"I thought you'd never ask."

The door flew open, and he had his clothes off by the time he reached the tub. "Is there room?"

"I'll make room."

And suddenly, every bad thought dissipated with the steam.

THE FOLLOWING MORNING, Heath edged out of bed, away from Willow's sleeping form. She still needed her rest. After every crazy thing that had happened to them yesterday, they both should've fallen into an exhausted sleep when they got back to the hotel. Instead, they'd made frantic, passionate love, as if to erase all the bad from their lives.

What had he said earlier? Their relationship, their attraction, seemed to be like a runaway train. And that train had gone off the rails last night.

He had to try to reach his father today. He couldn't keep the discovery of his mother's body to himself or wait for the confirmation. That locket told him everything he needed to know—well, not everything. He still didn't know what had happened to her or who put her in the ground.

His father deserved to hear this from him. Dad had suffered, too. He'd finally moved on with his life, with another woman, and they needed a chance for happiness with a clean slate. Nothing over their heads.

He left Willow a note, anchored by a bottle of ibuprofen and a promise to order her breakfast. She'd planned a nice, peaceful day hanging out at Astrid's and visiting the dogs. He'd take care of getting the key to her new storage unit and talking to West about Ellie's involvement in the campaign of terror against Willow.

Before he left the room, he kissed Willow on the forehead.

Back in his own room, he showered and changed clothes. Then he made the call he'd been dreading since yesterday. He used an app for a face-to-face call with his father.

The old man picked up on the first ring. "Son, it's good to finally hear from you...and see you. You look like hell. Told you that Dead Falls Island was always trouble. How's the deal going?"

"The deal is dead, Dad. Whether Lee Scott and his associates decide to go through with a smaller casino is up to them, but they're going to have to give up on the supporting infrastructure and tourist venues. Those two pieces of land are not for sale and never will be."

"I figured it was a long shot with the Tree Girl, but are Keel's niece and nephew not interested in making a bunch of money?"

"That's the thing, Dad. Paul Sands had some kind of deal in place that left the property to his daughter, Willow, after Keel passed. And that's what happened. She'll never sell."

His father blew a kiss to someone, presumably his wife, before turning back to his phone. "There is a little secret about that property that might just change her mind, Heath."

"It's not a secret, Dad. I found out about the mineral rights—*my* mineral rights. And I'm not going to threaten Willow with the exploitation of those rights to get her to sell for the lesser of two evils."

To his surprise, his father cracked a smile. "Still have a crush on that girl, huh?"

Heath's mouth gaped open for a few seconds. Who *didn't* know he'd had a crush on Willow back then, except Willow? "It's not just that. The island doesn't need any more development."

"Then that's it." His father ran a hand through his salt-and-pepper hair. "One thing I know after running this company for almost thirty years is you can't make people sell their property if they don't want to. Not worth it in the end."

"Th-there's something else, Dad."

"What? You're going to marry this girl?" He crooked his finger, and Heath's stepmother, Lilith, came into view, her head next to his father's.

"Hi, Heath. Are you getting married?"

The two of them giggled like a couple of teenagers.

He shook his head. "Not yet. What are you two doing right now?"

"Getting ready to have dinner and then a gondola ride. I know they're kitschy, but this is Lilith's first time in Italy. Have to do it right. If you're not getting married, what else were you going to tell me?"

Heath rubbed his thumb over the locket in his hand. "It can wait. Just wanted to let you know the deal's off and tell you I knew about the nickel vein. One thing, though."

"Fire away, but make it fast. The pasta here is singing to me."

"Do you know why Paul Sands signed those rights over to me?"

"No clue, son. I know he always felt sorry for you for some reason. Almost like he harbored some guilt when it came to you." He kissed his wife's fingers. "Gotta go. We'll meet when I get back."

Heath said goodbye to his father and Lilith and continued stroking the locket, as if it could give him answers. What did Paul Sands do to make him feel guilty?

His father took the news better than he'd expected him to take it. Marriage had softened his father's outlook. Lilith was young enough to be Dad's daughter, but she seemed to really care about him. She made him happy, and that had to count for something.

Heath texted Willow in case she was awake, but she didn't respond. He let her know he was on his way to pick up her storage unit key and talk to West about the lipstick found near her stolen bag.

As he grabbed a light jacket, his phone buzzed. Mark Santos's number flashed on the display. "Captain Mark, are you okay?"

"I'm madder than hell. I did *not* take any drugs before that flight. I didn't even have a beer."

"Is that what the tests are showing?"

"Tests are showing I had barbiturates in my system. No way. Didn't happen." He hacked a few times. "Just wanted to say I'm sorry about what went down, and I'm so thankful you were able to take over the controls. But I wasn't responsible for that mess."

"I believe you, Mark. Do you think someone drugged you?"

"Maybe. I have no idea who would want to or why, but I can't think of any other explanation for my condition."

"Are you out of the hospital? Can I come and talk to you today? I don't know the who, but I'm pretty sure about the why."

WILLOW BURROWED BENEATH the covers, reaching for the warmth of Heath's body. He'd been the cure she'd needed last night. How had she become so dependent on that man in such a short amount of time?

But her fingers met smooth, empty sheets, so she sat up suddenly, cradling her sore head. Squinting through sleep-encrusted lids, she spotted a square of white paper on the desk.

She inched out of bed to claim it, skimming over Heath's note. So, he'd take care of all the business today, and she'd relax at Astrid's with the dogs. She shook out an ibuprofen into her palm. She'd like to be there to see the look on Ellie's face when West questioned her.

She tossed the gel cap back with a gulp of water and thumbed through her text messages. Determined to make her day stress free, Heath had ordered her a breakfast of oatmeal with bananas, berries, nuts and almond milk. All she had to do was call room service to send it up.

Smiling, she ordered the breakfast and stepped into the bathroom for a quick shower. Different muscles ached this morning from the ones that throbbed with pain yesterday.

By the time she finished dressing and carefully removing the bandage from her head, room service knocked on the door. As she ate, she sent Heath a text thanking him for breakfast, or what had turned out to be lunch, and the other errands he was running on her behalf.

She stacked up the room service tray and fished her makeup bag from her purse. She often used the backpack purse when she had a lot of items to carry. Thankfully, she hadn't stuffed it last night on the way to the meeting.

She took a quick breath and pressed a hand to her chest. The recipe notebook. Hadn't she stashed that in her purse last night at the meeting? No. She'd left it in Heath's truck. Had wanted to show him then, but had gotten sidetracked giving him directions to the storage facility. She'd have to text him to remind him to bring it in with him when he finished his business...or her business.

Toby had to have a good reason for hiding that notebook beneath the floorboards, and it wasn't that he was planning to publish a cookbook and wanted to keep the recipes secret.

The hotel safe beckoned, and she checked the space in her bag. She had room for a gun, and after last night's adventure, she'd feel better with it—even at Astrid's with the dogs. She transferred the gun from the safe to her purse and hung it over a chair.

The sticky antiseptic from yesterday had created some clumps in her hair, so she pulled it into a ponytail. She grabbed her bag, patted the weapon inside and drove her truck to Astrid's. As she stepped out of her vehicle, Luna and Apollo charged toward her, Astrid's dog, Sherlock, trailing after them.

"It's dogpalooza!" Willow crouched down and wrapped her arms around the squirming mutts. "C'mon, Sherlock. You, too."

"They are so happy to see you."

Willow waved at Astrid, posed like a model on the porch that wrapped around the huge cabin. The place belonged to Astrid's brother, Tate, but she and her son had been staying with him for a while, and would continue to live here until Tate returned from an assignment in DC. Willow had a sneaking suspicion that Astrid and Olly would move in with West Chandler when Tate returned.

"You look nice," Willow told her. "Too nice for the rugged outdoors of Dead Falls."

Astrid made a face. "I know, sweetie. I'm sorry. I have a showing in town, and I have to leave. Don't worry. Olly is at his friend's house, and you can help yourself to anything in the fridge for lunch."

"No worries, Astrid. I'll hang out with the dogs. If I leave before you get back, do you want me to put them inside or leave them out?"

"Inside, please. When nobody's home, Sherlock still tends to wander."

"Got it, but if not today, let's catch up soon. I like the new sheriff." She flashed Astrid a thumbs-up. "I approve."

"I'm going to have a get-together when Tate comes home. I'll even invite Heath Bradford." Astrid gave her a broad wink. "Can you hold on to Sherlock while I run to my car? I don't want him jumping on my slacks."

Willow curled her fingers around Sherlock's collar. "I have him."

Astrid minced out to the Jeep in her high heels and beeped her horn when she drove away.

Willow settled in a chair at the edge of the firepit with a couple of balls and a knotted rope. Luna and Sherlock tussled and tumbled and chased the ball, while Apollo lazed contentedly at her feet.

She'd almost forgotten about the outside world when the dogs stopped their play and turned toward the woods, barking up a storm.

"Hey, get back here. You are not taking off on my watch, Sherlock." She grabbed a leash and corralled the big shepherd mix, leading him back to the house. "I'll give you some snacks inside, I'll have lunch, and then we'll resume our romp out here."

She didn't have to coerce the other two dogs. They scrambled after her and Sherlock, and she herded them inside the house.

About to step inside after the dogs, she heard a twig snap behind her and whirled around.

Garrett Keel raised a hand. "Hi, Willow. Got a minute?"

She licked her lips and considered releasing the dogs again, but her gaze flicked to her purse by the chair and the lump from her gun inside. She closed the door and stayed on the porch.

"Hey, Garrett. If you're coming here to put pressure on me or threaten me, give it up."

He slicked back his black hair. "I'm not my sister."

"What does that mean, Garrett?"

He aimed a toe, shod in an expensive cowboy boot, at a rock circling the firepit and then thought better of it. "Ellie has gone off the deep end. She's made some kind of devil's bargain with Lee Scott if she can deliver Uncle Toby's property. I—I'm worried about what she might do next."

Descending the porch as if approaching a wild animal, Willow said, "Is she responsible for the fire at my cabin? The airplane? My so-called mugging last night?"

Garrett pressed a clenched fist against his mouth. "Are you okay, Willow?"

"Is she trying to kill me?"

"She just wants to…convince you to see reason."

"That's not going to happen, Garrett." She edged a little closer to her purse. "And why are you here?"

"I want to get evidence against my sister once and for all. Put her where she belongs—in prison."

"Evidence against Ellie?" Willow spread her hands. "I don't have that. Just her lipstick and maybe a red flannel shirt—weak."

"I—I think you might have it, but you don't know it. Ellie's been searching for it."

"Searching for what? I didn't find anything in my father's papers—or Toby's, for that matter."

"Did you, by any chance, find a homemade recipe book? Handwritten recipes pasted inside a notebook with some food drawings on the cover?"

Willow's mouth dropped open. "I—I don't have it."

The pleasant mask dropped from Garrett's face as he took a menacing step toward her. "Don't lie to me, Willow."

Chapter Eighteen

Heath strode down the dock toward Mark Santos's boat and spotted Mark on the deck of a neat little Catalina 22 Sport. "Nice boat."

"Isn't she?" Mark patted the side. "Don't worry. I'm not going to set sail with you and pass out—unless you also know how to sail a boat."

"I do, but I'm not interested in taking over the controls again." Heath stepped onto the boat, joining Mark. "Tell me everything you remember."

"Took care of all my postflight duties and walked over to Seadog Pizza. They had a couple of games on the TVs there, so I ordered a pizza and a Coke. There were a few of my boating friends there, and we talked some smack for a while."

"Any strangers talk to you?"

"Of course. It's that kind of place—long tables, communal dining and drinking."

"Women?"

Mark cracked a grin. "Always."

"Any get close enough to your drink to slip you something?"

"Sure did. I even went to the john a few times and left my drink unattended. Don't they tell young ladies these days to take their drinks with them when they're in a bar? Should've followed that advice."

"Do you remember what any of these women looked like?"

"One particular blonde caught my eye. I even offered to take her up in my plane." Mark winked.

"No raven-haired sirens?"

"Could've been."

Heath fished his phone from his pocket and brought up a couple of photos he'd snatched of Ellie Keel from the internet. He turned his phone around to Mark. "Did you see her there?"

Mark shoved his sunglasses to the top of his head and squinted. "Naw, I don't think so."

Disappointed, Heath swiped to the next one. "How about this angle?"

Taking the phone from him, Mark brought it closer to his face and used his fingertips to zoom in. "Yeah."

"She was there?" Heath's pulse jumped. They needed all the evidence they could get against Ellie.

"Not the lady, man. The dude. That dude standing behind her was at the Seadog, all dressed up. Looked out of place."

Heath snatched the phone back from Mark and stared at Garrett Keel's face, enlarged. The two of them could be working together.

He smacked Mark on the back. "Thanks, man. I think we can get you cleared with the FAA. You were targeted and drugged."

A surprised Mark yelled his thanks as Heath clambered out of the boat. He had to tell Willow about this new development. He had no proof that Garrett Keel drugged Mark Santos, but they had a couple of starting points for West to dig his teeth into.

Back in his truck, he brought up Willow's texts to let her know about this latest development. He reread her text about the recipe book, and his gaze swept through the cab of his truck. The corner of the notebook peeked out from beneath the passenger seat, and he yanked on it.

As he pulled it free, several pages fell out of the middle of the book, and he gathered them in his hands. He glanced down at the loose pages and dropped them as if they'd scorched his hands.

He'd recognize his mother's handwriting anywhere.

"I'M NOT LYING, GARRETT. I don't have that notebook." Willow drew in her bottom lip, her gaze darting toward her purse.

He cleared his throat and looked at the sky. "I saw you with it at the meeting last night. You put it in your purse. I—I knew you were in trouble as soon as I saw it because I figured Ellie saw it, too. That's why she hit you and stole your purse. So if you just give it to me, you'll be safe from her."

From Ellie or from him?

"What's in that notebook, Garrett? It looked like recipes to me."

"So, you do have it. And you haven't read it. That's good. That'll keep you safe, Willow. Just give it to me, and I'll turn it over to Sheriff Chandler. It'll contain all the evidence he needs—against Ellie."

"What did Ellie do years ago that concerns the property and the casino project today? Why is Jessica Bradford's body buried behind Toby's cabin?"

Garrett's eyes bulged from their sockets. "How do you know that body is Jessica Bradford?"

"We know. Her son knows."

His face a bright red to match his sister's lipstick, Garrett screamed, "Where's the notebook, Willow?"

"It's right here, Garrett." Some branches at the tree line parted, and Heath stepped into the clearing. He raised the notebook in his hand. "I've got it right here... and I've read it."

Garrett staggered back a few steps, and then pulled a gun from his waistband. "Hand it over, Heath. Hand it over, or I'll shoot Willow, right here."

"I don't think you will, Garrett. You're not really a killer, are you? Despite what's in this booklet."

With Garrett's attention on Heath, Willow scooted closer to her purse, her foot inching toward the strap on the ground.

"It's a lie, Heath. I didn't kill your mother. Toby did."

Willow froze. "You killed Heath's mother?"

Heath spread his arms, still clutching the notebook. "You were right, Willow, except it wasn't Toby who came on to my mom. It was Garrett. She rebuffed him. Laughed at him, even, for his youth. Enraged, he tried to assault her, but she fought back. He shoved her, and her head cracked against a rock. An accident, right, Garrett? An accident during the commission of another crime."

"She was using Uncle Toby. She had an unhappy marriage, and she cried on Uncle Toby's shoulder. I told her she could cry on my shoulder anytime. I meant that. I loved your mother."

Heath snarled, "Stop! Your uncle helped you. You both buried her in the back, and Toby told everyone how suicidal she was, how she wanted to disappear and spare her family the grief. He may have even planted that note we found. But Toby wrote it all down, appended to my mother's own diary of events. He kept it in case you ever tried to turn things on him. In case you ever tried to get his property from Willow's dad."

"Willow's dad." Garrett spit out the words. "He knew what happened."

Willow covered her mouth. "My father knew what happened to Jessica?"

Garrett sneered. "That's why he left the mineral rights to her son. Guilt."

"He suspected, Willow." Heath shook the notebook. "He didn't know for sure. He just suspected."

Willow's gut churned. "So, you wanted your uncle's land to *stop* the development so nobody would ever find Jessica Bradford?"

Garrett threw back his head and laughed. "That's my sister's thing. I don't give a damn about this land, never did. But when my uncle threatened to expose me, I'd had enough."

Willow swallowed. "You did kill Toby."

Garrett's voice grew whiny. "It was an accident. The old fool was going to die anyway. His doctor had given him months. He wanted to come clean, clear his conscience— at my expense. I knew he'd invited Bradford over to tell him the truth. We argued. He fell."

"Just like my mother, huh?" Heath said. "People have a habit of falling around you and dying."

Willow taunted, "You should've waited until you found out where Toby kept the diary before killing him."

"I know." Garrett wiped his forehead with the back

of his hand. "When I discovered you inherited the property, Willow, I had to step up my game and search everything. I even drugged the dogs to get access, but I never would've killed them. I'm not a killer. Just in case it was in your place, I set fire to it. I would've torched Toby's place eventually. Guess I was too late."

Folding his arms, Heath clamped the diary against his body. "And the airplane? Mark Santos just ID'd you as being in the pizza place that day. I said before that you weren't a killer, but maybe you just like to do it at a distance or all by accident."

Garrett shrugged, and the gun wavered. "I knew you were going to San Juan Island to look up the mineral rights on the property. I saw an opportunity to take out both of you at the same time. Nobody else would be interested in a diary stuffed inside a cookbook. The mystery would've died with you two."

As Garrett turned his attention to Heath, Willow gestured toward her purse with fingers formed into a gun. Heath gave a quick shake of his head.

Heath coughed and spoke loudly. "What about Ellie? Is she involved in all this?"

"I planted her lipstick by Willow's purse when I dumped it just to shift the suspicion and buy myself time." Garrett snorted. "Not that she didn't enjoy the attacks on Willow. She might've suspected me of those attacks, but she never asked me directly. Like I said, she's all about this land deal. She's having an affair with Lee Scott and will do just about anything…"

While Garrett rambled, his attention on Heath and the notebook in his hand, Willow had snagged the strap of her purse with her foot. It now lay at her feet.

As she started to dip, Heath yelled out and tossed the notebook in the air. "Here you go, Garrett!"

Garrett lunged toward the notebook, still clutching the gun and waving it in her direction.

While Willow scrabbled for the weapon in her purse, Heath charged Garrett, knocking him to the ground. Garrett's gun went off, and Willow screamed.

She pulled her own gun from her purse and hopped up. She aimed it toward the two men rolling on the ground, grappling for agency over the weapon in Garrett's hand.

She ran toward them, her gun shaking. She'd never killed a living thing in her life and didn't know if she could do it now. She yelled, "Stop! I have a gun."

Garrett jerked his head in her direction, and Heath's knee cracked down on his wrist. The gun popped from his grasp, and Willow grabbed it.

As Garrett cowered on the ground, Heath jumped up and loomed above him, fists clenched. "I should kill you for what you did to my mother."

Willow stumbled back from him. A gun in each hand, she put them behind her back. "He's not worth it, Heath."

Garrett started laughing and choking, rolling onto his side. "This island. I hate this island."

Epilogue

Astrid yelled, "Olly, I'm gonna tell you one last time—you and your friends take the dogs in the back and get them away from the food."

A gaggle of boys ran to the back of Astrid's cabin, the three dogs passing them on the way.

Astrid came around with a bottle of wine and refilled everyone's glasses. "So, Garrett started this whole thing by killing his uncle over that diary, but by killing him he also cut off his only chance of finding the diary. Genius."

Heath crooked his fingers in air quotes. "'Accidentally' killed him, just like my mother."

"I'm so sorry about your mother, Heath." Astrid sat beside West and took his hand.

West said, "Forensics is still waiting for her dental records. I'm sorry, too, Heath. I don't know what kind of game Toby Keel was playing."

"I don't think Toby was a very good guy." Willow sniffed. "And I'm not sure about my father, either."

Stroking her arm, Heath said, "Garrett said your father had his suspicions but didn't know for sure."

"He left you the mineral rights to that property based on a suspicion?" Willow took a gulp of wine. "I don't think so."

"You know what I think?" Astrid raised a finger in the air. "I think your father knew about the mutual, un-expressed attraction between the two of you and left Heath those rights to bind you together forever."

"My father, the hopeless romantic." Willow snorted. "I doubt it."

"It's my fiancée who's the hopeless romantic." West twirled a lock of Astrid's blond hair around his finger. "Willow, is Ellie Keel still planning to sue you for the property?"

Willow answered, "I think she's going to drop the idea, just like Lee Scott dropped her. Lee didn't want any connection to the Keels after Garrett's arrest."

"Lee's also putting a hold on developing the Samish plot for the casino." Heath scooped a hand through his hair. "Too much attention, too much bad publicity."

Tilting her head, Willow asked, "How does your father feel about that?"

"Talk about old romantics—my father has new pri-orities since getting married."

"You hear that?" West leveled a finger at Astrid and then touched her nose. "After we get married, my pri-orities might change."

"Uh-oh, I thought I already was your number one pri-ority." Astrid dragged his finger to her lips and kissed the tip. Hearing a yelp from the back of the house, Astrid jumped to her feet. "I don't know if that was boy or dog, but we're going to check on both and start cleaning up."

She waved her hand as Willow started to rise. "You two, relax. You deserve it."

Willow sat back down and scooted her chair closer to Heath's until their knees touched. "How'd your father take the news of the discovery of your mother's burial site?"

"He's still waiting on the verification of the dental records, but I told him about the locket. Told him the whole story of Garrett Keel's obsession with her." Heath hunched forward and took her hands. "He was sad. Felt like a failure as a husband all over again, but there's a sense of relief there, too."

"And you? Have you processed all this yet?"

"Selfishly, I feel vindicated in my belief that my mom never would've up and left us with no explanation."

"That's not selfish." She leaned forward and kissed him. "And how about this island? You used to love it. Do you hate it now? Feel like it's cursed?"

He traced a finger along her jaw. "I loved the island because it reminded me of the Tree Girl. It still does. And now I own a piece of it, below the dirt where the mist meets the earth. I'll love any place the Tree Girl calls home...as long as she'll let me."

"I guess we do have a deal, then, Son, because the Tree Girl loves you where the mist meets the earth and anywhere else."

* * * * *

If you missed the previous books in Carol Ericson's
A Discovery Bay Novel series, they're available now!
You'll find these titles wherever Harlequin Intrigue
books are sold:

Misty Hollow Massacre
Point of Disappearance
Captured at the Cove